A WERESHARK'S MEMOIR II

A Wereshark's Memoir II

JUSTIN T. O'CONOR SLOANE

Wild Man
of the
Woods
Press

This
book is dedicated
to
all of those for whom
the
imagination
is
the greatest exploration,
they
who run hard against
the
oppressive, global monolith
of
bureaucratic-corpocratic-data-point-driven
systems of thought
that
assign little value
and
even less importance to
the
first wonder of the world,
the
human imagination.
You
know who you are.
This
book is for
you.

ISBN: 979-8-9925058-0-1

Text © 2025 by Justin T. O'Conor Sloane

Editor & publisher, Justin T. O'Conor Sloane
Cover art: *Tempest on the Sea at Night* (1849)
by Ivan Konstantinovich Aivazovsky
Book design by Katerina von Brüno

Wild Man of the Woods Press
an imprint of
Starship Sloane Publishing Company, Inc.
Austin-Round Rock, Texas

starshipsloane.com

PRAISE FOR A WERESHARK'S MEMOIR

"In his magnum opus *Ethics* published posthumously in 1677, Spinoza argues that God is substance. Evil is substance in *A Wereshark's Memoir* by Justin Sloane. Original, frightening, and beautiful, this work is a study into the impossibility of evil to reign over the human race. It is a fiction of the open wound. It hurts and it makes you invent a therapy to alleviate pain. Often this is impossible. In a way, it is a subtle analysis of what society suffers from today. As Justin Sloane puts it, 'Time is neither friend nor foe. But it can be made either.'"

—Zdravka Evtimova, 4x best novel of Bulgaria and author of *He May Wear My Silence*

"With all the linguistic beauty of scientific romance, and a splash of cosmic horror, Mr. Sloane takes us on an aquatic romp through piracy, love, and death. Fans of William Hope Hodgson will want to devour this tale."

—Jean-Paul L. Garnier, editor of *Star*Line* magazine and author of *Garbage In, Gospel Out*

"Justin Sloane's *A Wereshark's Memoir* is a true megalodon of a novella, howling hammerheaded through the centuries, timeless like that eldest breed named for Greenland. Equal parts werewolf, shark, and swashbuckler who befriends Blackbeard himself, Sloane's narrator, sea-bewitched, bioluminescent shapeshifter, proves at least as haunted as a Ulysses unable ever to return home."

—Dr. Matt Schumacher, editor of *Phantom Drift: A Journal of New Fabulism* and author of *The Fire Diaries: Poems*

CONTENTS

PREFACE

It had been a while since I entertained my interest in the world of pirates, always a favorite subject of mine, so I sailed back into it with gusto! The surname Sloane (Ó Sluaghadháin) means "raider" in Gaelic, so maybe it's in the blood.

I was inspired to write this story when I learned that Richard Grieco was working on a new movie, *Time Pirates*, and that he was playing the fearsome pirate, Blackbeard. I've been a fan of Richard's acting since tuning in each week to watch *21 Jump Street*. It turns out that he's also a talented and accomplished visual artist. I've had the honor of publishing some of Richard's work over the years in various literary journals and magazines of Starship Sloane Publishing.

Interestingly enough, I once worked with a guy who claimed to be a descendant of Edward Thache Jr., better known as Edward "Blackbeard" Teach. I have no reason to doubt my colleague's claims of ancestry but for his exceptionally pacific disposition. Nevertheless, he was a fearless racecar driver and I think that must have been where he channeled his latent, piratical ferocity. I once went along for a ride with him on an improbably twisting road through the aspirationally nicknamed Issaquah Alps near Seattle and aged at least ten years during that infernal terror ride—one that would have made Blackbeard himself proud and would likely have flared his fuses into a full conflagration.

The photo in my author bio was taken in Boston, one of my favorite cities. So much history there. That's some part of Boston Harbor behind me. I graduated from high school in the Boston area and used to go into the city from time to time, occasionally taking the "T" on all-day tours, during which I always paid a visit to the United States Coast Guard recruiting office. While in high school, I took a navigation & seamanship class that included a boat tour of Boston Harbor which lit up my sea-faring senses and a marine science class that included a fieldtrip to our town's shoreline and its tide pools. While growing up in California, visits to San Francisco, Monterey and Fort Bragg inspired a great love of the sea. But the defining moment was in Connecticut, along the Long Island Sound, watching in awe as my aunt cut the motor and spun the ship's wheel of her sailboat, gliding the elegant craft masterfully into its slip in the marina. I was all set to join the Coast Guard but was ultimately shipped off to college in the redwoods of California instead, though I could still see the ocean from the highest point on campus. Later, living in Seattle for many years, I was deeply enamored with the Puget Sound. I suppose that I am a thalassophile who actually prefers the mountains but lives near neither. Ah, well, c'est la vie. In a very real sense, this story, like any good ship, has been long in the build.

This novella is the greatly expanded version of the novelette published in 2024 which was in turn the greatly expanded version of the short story that I originally wrote for the debut issue of *The Lotus Tree Literary Review*, winning first place in the 25th Annual Critters Readers' Poll in the science fiction & fantasy short story category.

I still think that there is much more that could be written in this story as it follows a free flow of fantastical imagination and so there are really no limitations as to where it might ultimately make its journey, but I do consider it to be complete . . . once again . . . at least for the time being.

Thank you for being here. I sincerely hope that you enjoy the story. Sail into your richly deserved literary adventure—but beware the odd wereshark lurking about.

Justin
26 January 2025
Deep in the heart of Texas

PART I

I AM A WERESHARK

I will say this before I begin in proper. My substance is best understood when measured in nautical miles of stealth and plunder. My history, the moon and the sea. My legend, a jewel of blood and saltwater.

This is my story.

I am a wereshark. We don't receive as much notice as our landlocked brethren. Granted, there are far more of them, we being a rarer breed indeed.

I have met only two others of my kind in all these centuries, not including young Teach in whose fate I played a role. Both far older than I and far more powerful. I was wise to stay a hemisphere away. They had progressed to a phantasmal state of bioluminescence when transformed. I found that to be most interesting. A menacing beauty. An expression of the moon and sea that wrought us.

My ancestors left Connacht in the west of Éire as the last of the high kings fell, the might of that ancient bloodline washing away with the rain into the moss and lichen, down through the rocks to the sea, as the storm and sword of a new and terrible history rolled dark across that distant green altar, my Emerald Isle. For generations we roamed the coasts of the continent. Working as fishermen, seafarers, and shipwrights. A maritime legacy. I have never returned to the wild sea and green hills of Ireland. And I never will.

The sea has been my bright paradise, and it has been my darkest prison. It has been my joy, and it has been my torment. I have lived the sea like a salt-mad sailfish in the wind. To be a seaman, riding the currents, the winds, and the waves, has provided a measure of peace and camaraderie, grand adventure, and treasure beyond my most fevered dreams. It has also brought me notoriety—in which I once reveled. But to be a wereshark, in eternal bondage to the sea, has been a life unasked for.

Aqua. An axehard word for a substance soft and evaporative-ethereal. Terra firma. Ah, its peaceful sanctuary has done me much good, this recovering thalassophile.

Trees, now, my mast and sail, moss and lichen, my barnacled hull, fields of wind-driven grass, my green waves, meadows of wildflower abstraction, my coral reefs, still bogs, my saltwater lagoons, and always, the most delicious smell of rain.

Till the full moon calls me, as inescapably as it does the tides, to the sea.

The carnage, the sea-dog ferocity, the blood and saltwater, I am transmogrified, a shark and a man, with an almost human mind, but clouded, drugged, crazed, a thirst for blood of the sea drives me.

Once ashore, I go far from the seaside, deep into the mountains. A vegan with an almost hysterical aversion to seafood and any dish that once had blood. I say that I have allergies. I have become a solitary wanderer of forests and valleys, deserts and jungles. I follow legends and myths now, no longer the winds and currents of the Seven Seas. I search for the Seven Cities of Cibola and the many other lost cities of gold. I will find El Dorado one day, if it indeed exists. I search for the hoards of treasure cloaked in the mists of time. I search for the relics of rumor but find only whispers on the wind. I seek the unknown. The eternally hidden. The mysteries, the lore, the tales told around campfires and pints. I seek the lotus tree of Homer and Ovid. I have the time, so much time, and the blood-stained wealth to do as I wish. In truth, this is all just my entertainment, for I seek something else. Something greater, far greater. I traveled the Seven Seas long. Always looking for it. My crew as well, though they may not have realized. And I am still. That which sparkles and glitters, shining in a light all its own, far beyond any earthly riches. More splendid than all the treasure piled high and cascading of this material world. I didn't find it then. Though all of the many who were once my crew across the centuries, save Blackbeard, have. That I know. My command means nothing to them now. I am no longer their captain. The quick of sword and the bold of deed. They have another. But I seek it always. And I will never find it. This I also know. Such is the life of a wereshark. Such is not the life of a man or woman mere and mortal. Growing like wildflowers do, climbing their yellowshine trestle of sunlight into the blue and blossoming air, only to slowly fall, grayed and stooped with age, into the earth again. I live on.

I made my fortune long ago, aboard a swift ship of which I was the captain. Her name, the *Ximena Feroz*. A ship good and true. We were salt-flocked wolves of the sea, marauders drawn by mighty sails. The winds and the waves, leading us by their design, to each new opportunity in the glorious Age of Sail. There will never be another like it. Great sailing ships of discovery and commerce navigating the waters of the world. Sailing forth into the sun and the moon and the stars. Plying the known and charting the new. The future was ours. We would sail into it with sea salt in our beards and rum in our throats. A burning for treasure in our hearts. A most golden adventure it would be. The seagoing senses so alive. Salt air in the lungs and the symphony of wind on sail, mast, and wave. The fragrance of the sea, an elixir to the soul. The movement of wood on water, a meditation. The dance of wood and wave, a magic. The spray of the salted sea, a daily baptism. The compass rose and the mariner's astrolabe emblazoning my dreams. We sailed beneath the glory-bright heavens. We sailed on effervescence through the sparkling seas of crystalline sun showers. We sailed beneath skies of the highest blue and those that fluoresced green. We sailed above waters of the deepest blue and those that engulfed green. We saw things that could not be readily understood and others that gripped us by the back of the neck in the dead of night. We saw phantoms gliding at sea, spectral ships, an assortment of ghost lights that floated about, dissipating into the dark of night, and strange, glowing orbs that darted about and encircled the ship, blinking in and out of view, all of them like will-o'-the-wisps of the sea—that sometimes emerged from the sea itself, and tiny phosphorescent water sprites dancing on the crests of waves. We heard the songs, weeping, and laughter of the sylphs, just at the edge of perception, murmuring on the winds and echoing in the sails. Women's voices gently called to us, rising from the troughs and from just beyond the swells. And at times, a tapping on the hull, that chilled us to the very marrow. Merfolk swam near the ship, vanishing as pale-green shadows beneath the surface. Creatures that shivered the timbers of our ship and great, barnacled tentacles that slapped the deck, and trailing seaweed, slid back into the depths. Coral reefs reflecting like great, bejeweled necklaces dropped by the sea giants of old. Storms that shook our bones and blinded our souls. Days that were but twilight. And seas that glowed blue at night. Whalesong, our strange lullaby from the deep.

Moments of high adventure that made me forget what I had become. Moments of riotous fun that shone bright the grand spectacle of life. An occasion found us surrounded by a roiling arribada of sea turtles so dense and vast that my landing party could not use the jolly boats, they hopped and reeled wildly across the great bubbling, carbonation of carapaces to the shore. I had nearly fainted with bullroar laughter. And there were moments of absolute tranquility. The embrace of a dense fog on a serene sea was to ascend into the silent, white cathedral of the clouds themselves. And the sea was my cathedral. It was my worship. And it was my captor.

We once came upon a long-dead man crucified in the Roman fashion, a near-skeletal vision of a Christ at sea, the cross affixed to a great log raft. He rode the waves like a grinning scarecrow, disappearing into the troughs and leaping out at us atop his cresting craft, as though playing a sinister game of peekaboo. Those of my men who still felt the weight of religion on their soul, muttered prayers to the Redeemer and trembling, made the sign of the cross. At my hoarse command, we grappled his craft to ours, poured lamp oil over the side and sent him off as a torch aflame. It was then I first took notice that the spars of my ship formed crosses, and I, in my darkest, most fiendish hours of sea-wrought madness, had men nailed high about, leaving them to return in bits to the deck below. Though my most inspired was to become known as the Devil's Shish Kabob. I will provide no details here. Whether such wickedness was born of my own heart or of the unholy abomination I had been made into, I do not rightly know.

By the Golden Age of Piracy, I had long since become a legend of the high seas. When in battle, it was said that my face blazed as fire, that I moved as a quick flame, consuming all before me. I was called Captain of the Wine-Red Hand. And at times, simply, the Red Captain. My emerald-hilted cutlass was whispered of from the Bosporus Strait to the Indian Ocean. It was boasted that using just one of the Apostles from around my waist, I could both shave the skinny whiskers off a man at spyglass distance with my pistol and fillet a flying fish right into the galley cook's pan. I was that very seaborne plague that begat a perpetual fear. The Jolly Roger, as it came to be known by the bastard English, was the rum-soaked work of my own artistic hand and to none we met, jolly. I was no Mither o' the Sea. My men knew hard well that when the full moon rose, safety could only be found far aloft in the rigging, the nearer to St. Elmo's Fire the better, he, the patron saint of sailors. On more than one occasion, a lad of my crew had slipped from the yards, plummeting like a diving seabird, at the sight of my moonlit form. My agelessness was a subject of suspicious wonder and mystery to all who did not know my true nature. Mariners told the tale that under a red sky at morning, I had gained immortality by offering a ship laden with fleur de sel, its sails washed burgundy with the blood of my foes, to the crimson-embered devil himself. And that soon thereafter, a screaming tempest had brought a red and boiling, sulfurous sea. Steam and vapor rose high, and "AYE" was writ large in the foul air for all to see. The bargain had been accepted. The contract signed in brimstone and saltwater, as it were. My eternal youth and the exploits attributed to me were taken as incontrovertible proof of that most vile transaction.

I have been called a privateer, a corsair, a buccaneer, a freebooter, and a pirate—depending on time and place and occasional employ. I have been called the Saltwater Devil, the Devil's Own Squall, and even the Devil of the Sea. In fact, I have been called everything but a child of God. Verily, multitudes were the ship that found itself between the devil and the deep blue sea as my dread crew and I drew nigh. I have made many the man, good and bad alike, walk the plank and I have keelhauled many more. I was no pleasantry then as now. I have taught a legion of riches-hungry souls the ways of a plundering life at sea down through the ages. Young Teach, who came to braid fuses into his black beard, got his start under my command and owes me his life, then and still. My ship was never lost, never captured, but freely given upon my departure from the daily sea.

It is a quiet life for me now. And secretive, as it has long been. Red wine and rum, too much, and poetry, too little. An earnest splash of paint here and there. Reminding me that I'm no Pollack. Some classical music, a new pleasure in the days of yore. I once ordered my men to capture a squeaking man and his gleaming harpsichord. We lashed them securely to the foremast and had the music of a palace court at sea for a time. But full moon comes calling, a sinister carnival barker levitating bright aglow. I plan ahead, renting Lambos and Ducatis, flooring them to the coast. This fish-to-be can drive like Mario Andretti—and ride a bike, too. Diving deep from cliff tops, displaying expert technique, a lycanthropene

Greg Louganis. I'm more dorsal fin than man by three strokes in. Neptune deliver whatever I might find down there. I once catapulted myself upon a scuba club on their annual full-moon dive—a fundraising event for endangered sea turtles. One of their imprinted snorkels washed ashore in Fiji five years later, cocooned in sea life, and made the international news. A flipper, bite mark and all, had been found in a tide pool halfway to Santa Monica and a chewed-up diving suit-come-suborbital-projectile, gyrating as a windsock from a coastal cypress one county over. It was as though a crate of toothy TNT had detonated right in the middle of their little soirée in the sea. I can't help but chuckle. Many the surfer has escaped my terrible jaws as I laughed uncontrollably beneath the waves, green-eyed tears to the sea, watching them paddle furiously in a swell of profound and pissing terror. I don't feel guilty anymore. I do what I am. I didn't ask to become this cursed creature of the fathomless marine, those many centuries long ago, along that moonlit Sicilian coastline.

It was my honeymoon and my last moments as a mortal man. Memories of my sweet wife haunt me still. I walked on the beach as she slept, her long black hair flowing from the bed, swaying gently as kelp in the sea breeze. I had gazed out upon the shimmering, hypnotic expanse of the night sea from our balcony. Felt the gravity of the heavy moon pulling at my blood and was drawn to the surf in a swoon. Each receding wave calling me closer. I enjoyed the feel of cool sand between my toes and the lapping of seawater at my ankles. The sweeping flash and long eclipse of a far distant lighthouse spoke a peculiar mixture of comfort and solitude as I walked luxuriously in the ancient histories of Mediterranean civilization. It's sunken ships, battles between warring empires on the sea, and explorers sailing forth to shape destiny enveloped me as fully as any sea mist would. The full moon, that most radiant goddess, or so I once thought of her, watered my eyes, so low I could have reached out for a pinch of moon dust. I drank cognac from the bottle my wife and I had bought in Corsica and reveled in my joy on that splendid shoreline. Smoking Spanish tobacco long in transit, the fragrance of a new world, I had been making bold and daring plans for a seafaring future. Horror sometimes finds you when you least expect it. And least deserve it. I never saw her again, my raven-haired wife, but it is just as well. For I am a demon. Moon spawn of sea foam and dark waves. A pale demon of the deep blue sea. What other am I? And she, a saint. A saint of the calm depths, the currents, and the churning whitecaps. My patroness saint, Saint of the Seven Seas. The keeper of a sacred ember of light in the distant altar of my mind. The saint of my most hallowed memories.

~ II ~

ROBIGUS

A nd so it is. A solitary life. Forlorn even.
And I have searched . . . relentlessly . . . for any
information that I can find concerning my wife. Our honeymoon cut short by the cruel timing of my transformation on that moonlit Sicilian shore so long ago. I employ historians to scour archival records abroad but have yet to find anything but the pale dust of old sorrows. It is a void in my soul. Through which a cold and screaming wind blows. This is all I will say in the matter.

But what of Blackbeard you may ask? He pays me a visit from time to time. He is the respected captain of a merchant ship now. His pirating history has been very well chronicled, but his current identity is unknown. Great wealth can buy almost anything, in his case, a new life. One with the respect of society and with professional dignity. He's become a devout Christian. One would never know now the terrors he once wrought. Like rain on a roof, it has flowed away, been absorbed and obscured, and become something new. New life. Like leaves sprouting from branches. I am happy for him. He, as I, had not asked for this fate. He, as I, was not deserving of this fate. But, in the grand scheme of things, deserving and receiving are two entirely unrelated things. I know that now. As does he. As the days of pirating—at least as we knew them to be—came to an end, we had agreed to scuttle the *Ximena Feroz*, that finest of ships, rather than let any other use her for anything other than what had long been her destiny proud, that of a feared and magnificent pirating ship of such superb elegance and trusted seaworthiness that she had won a fame unknown to any other sailing ship. It took me many long years to finally dry my tears. Blackbeard, too. We loved that fierce ship like life itself. As it sank beneath the waves, so too, sank our hearts, and when it vanished from view, so too, the lives we had known. Forevermore. It was then a time of reinvention for Blackbeard. The time had come for him to begin writing a new chapter in his life's story. I was already writing mine. But when our ship no longer sailed the seas, resting beneath, so too the inklines of destiny dried in their clear finality. Forward. Only forward. Our past lies beneath the bluegreen waves of the sea.

I have removed myself from the tyranny of daily chores and mundane concerns. I hire many to do much. I have also endeavored to extricate myself from social obligations and interactions to the greatest extent possible. I desire neither society nor what it offers, beyond its ability to support the freedoms of my lifestyle.

I have at times trekked north to revel in the aurora borealis. Commissioning a pilot, I drop from on high in a glider, sailing silently through the swirling green spectacle spilling about the atmosphere like great rivers of light flowing from the heavens. This reminds me greatly of my days at sea. It brings me that same sense of expansive joy and adventure, but as it is not the sea, I do not feel bound to it. It is an exhilarating freedom that I experience in these precious moments.

In much the same way, during the rise of a full moon I once barreled a vast and tubular silverbright beam of its light piercing anthracite clouds many hundreds of stories thick. My timing was precisely executed and I transmogrified in view of the white caps below, ditching the glider in a controlled frenzy and diving deep into the intoxicating Pacific, a dark and dazzling pool of undulating moonshine.

I have battled the giant Pacific octopus in the cold, dark depths of Puget Sound, their skin a raging red and have given orcas far more than they bargained for. Great whites see me as their own and so I have not yet had the pleasure of combat with their ilk.

I have noticed that I too, have begun to luminesce, just as I had seen the other two of my kind do, they far older and more powerful than I. I will someday terminate their hemispheric reign. The same may come to pass one day with Blackbeard, but I would prefer to think that we should remain friends. There need not be only one.

I have endeavored with the ironmost will of discipline for centuries now to develop the powers of telekinesis. My thinking in the matter is that with enough time and focused meditation, plumbing the greatest depths of the mind and exploring its most remote and uncharted properties and potential, that I should be able to achieve this objective, that I should be able to manifest this power if it is indeed possible, as some would suggest. I have not yet succeeded. But I will not let my disappointment in this practice dissuade me from continuing to try.

I do notice though that I have an exceptionally heightened sense of perception, I would venture to say that it borders on being ESP, or that it may even be ESP. This is an exciting possibility to me, but I cannot yet differentiate between the possibility that it is the heightened senses of a shark driving this ability or if it originates independently. Time, meditation, and deeply intuitive processes of the mind will eventually lead me to the answers I seek.

As an entertainment, I purchased a balloon capable of reaching the stratosphere. I had seen a Swiss man by the name of Piccard do just such a thing. It inspired me and focused my energies externally for a time. I trained in its piloting and set off to enjoy this newfound and grand sport. I had been impatient in my learning and training and had made many errors in calculation, including that of duration. I had not even bothered to hire a ground control, thinking that my experience as a captain in great gales and typhoons would have prepared me for anything. A balloon is not a sailed ship and my conceits in the matter faded as quickly as the ground beneath me. I was not as good with the instrumentation as

I should have been. I would soon learn the error of my ways. A lesson in humility and baffled helplessness that I required but once to become a much wiser being. Forethought and careful preparation are the keys to success in any endeavor, of which I was pointedly reminded. As I gained great elevation events began to unfold in a decidedly contrary fashion to what I had planned and I was not able to descend. To begin with, the winds of the upper atmosphere behave far differently than the saltwater-kissed winds of the sea. They are also as cold as any cube of ice. And they never subside. Drawing you along streams of air that circle the globe. Much time passed. Then much more. As I drifted over the western Pacific Ocean one night I was shocked to see the full moon present itself mightily. I had been high adrift for many days and had paid no attention to the phases of the moon, being so utterly immersed in the details of my instrumentation and attempting to overcome my deficit of training in piloting a high-altitude balloon. I felt the frenzy come upon me. It seemed more powerful than usual, perhaps being closer to the moon energized the transformation in a way that I had not yet experienced. The frenzy soon hit such a fevered pitch that I had lost all sense of reason. Beyond that, the change was happening far more quickly and the need to be in saltwater became more urgent than it had ever been before. Unable to descend, traveling at a tremendous speed through the frigid sky, inexorably transforming within the gondola, I became a berserker, tearing the cockpit to pieces and ripping the entry portal from its hinges. A split second later, I was free falling through the atmosphere, plummeting towards the ocean at such an extreme velocity that I was reintroduced to a long-forgotten emotion: fear. A giddying and unrelenting fear that soon evaporated into a kind of strange euphoria. I did not know if I could survive such a fall, even when fully transformed, which I now was. But I knew that I needed to knife into the water if I were to have any chance at all. Through a series of furious contortions and maneuvers I managed to align myself as a diver would, entering the water moments later with a cracking boom. My body, violently shuddered by the slicing impact, stung as though engulfed by 10,000 hornets. I blacked out a moment later. How long I was unconscious I do not know. But when I awoke I knew myself to be many leagues deeper than I had ever been. I could feel a great pressure surrounding me, pushing in on me, unlike anything I had previously experienced. I was slowly drifting deeper, in a gentle swaying motion like that of a hammock, looking up through the black of the water, my eyes unable to focus on anything. I felt a sudden surge of claustrophobia shimmer through my being and a strobing confusion; both of these were also alien and long-forgotten sensations. I knew that I needed to take action and begin swimming to regain my sense of equilibrium and agency. I shot upwards with a white-hot and blazing fury of purpose. Soon, light began to diffuse the water as the surface drew nearer. I relaxed my efforts and began zigzagging horizontally in a leisurely fashion. In command of my senses once more and feeling like any other shark of the sea again, I smiled a toothy grin through the dark-green water and set off to pursue a meal. Later, calculating my estimated velocity, the coefficient of friction, and the density of water, among other factors, I came to understand that I had managed to thread the needle and plunge many leagues deep into the Mariana Trench itself. I have not gone near a balloon of any size since.

Through devices of the most exquisite cunning and subterfuge, I have managed to lure werewolves to the shores of the sea, whereupon, I have pulled them beneath the surf in a flash and ripped them asunder. Paying no heed to what they may have been in their daily lives. If they were accountants in the light of the sun, then ledgers will go untabulated. And thus it will be. The were-life is a dangerous one indeed and I have a deep and abiding hatred for those hairy, howling beasts. As I have stated, I am no pleasantry.

My memories besiege me, yet they are all that I have really. They define me.

Once, while floating the windless, infinite blues and browns of the Sargasso Sea, a great glowing craft descended silently from the starbright heavens and took a deckhand away with it through a strange apparatus of silver light, up through which the poor lad rose against his best efforts, Newton's apple but contrary to the intentions of nature. We fired our pistols at the craft as it tarried about our masts and managed a volley from the cannons as it flew slowly around us in an ever-widening circle, then flashed from sight at a speed the likes of which we had no ken and that left our eyes moist with the dew of a sober disbelief and our faces irrigated by the anxious rivulets of water that flowed freely from our brows. I quickly decided upon the appropriate course of action to find our pirating bearings, grog be damned, I ordered fresh barrels of rum brought topside from the spirit room and we drank for hours upon end, singing rowdy songs til every man jack stumbled to his hammock below decks or slid to his boots and slept in the velvety seabreeze of sugarcane fields distilled into firenectar on the not distant islands of the Caribbean.

Moving through swaying kelp forests, made aglow with shafts of moonlight, an illumination of ethereal green, I find tranquility within my animal self for some brief moments at a time. But like a racehorse out of the gates, I'm soon rushing forward to seek new carnage.

When I think of what the ocean has consumed and created through its systems of digestion and renewal through the many millions of years, I know myself to be as inconsequential as any grain of sand on its shores. A cosmos of sand reflected within a cosmos of stars. But, this I also know. That I must therefore make my own meaning, through the consequence of my mind, ideas and personal philosophy manifested through the action of my hands into a physical reality. This is what my God requires of me. It is not the God of the many, it is my God. My God alone. No explanation necessary, no converts desired, no like-minded connections with others sought. I am a wereshark. Few of us exist, no two really alike. No mortal capable of meeting us where we are. And so. And so, I am the sum total of the spirituality of my own God. I am the past, the present, and the future. I am the chosen one. I am the disciple. It serves me well.

I enter the great Christian cathedrals from time to time. To try to feel that expression of the divine. It does not supplant my God. I had once thought myself beyond the shadow of religion, yet I have become my own religion. A strange irony, I suppose.

The Galápagos Islands, were to me the most enchanted of archipelagos. The Enchanted Isles. More so than any other. The Tortoise Islands, their very name. I saw in their volcanic proclamation the very processes whereby life migrated from the sea to the land. A severity of rock and a profusion of unique creatures that I had not glimpsed elsewhere. Giant tortoises like ambling, green haystacks and enormous, black lizards with vibrant, green patches that swam and dove beneath the waves and those that were of the brightest citrus yellows and oranges, while others still, were a hellish pink, scrambling across a primordial landscape hot as the devil's own soul. And boobies, but with bright blue feet, as though dipped in the finest of artists' paint. And none had a fear of man in them. A source of their demise. We cooked tortoises in the great cauldron of their own shell over bonfires aflash with spilled rum and fanciful tales and celebrated our hardy-good fortune. We provisioned great quantities of fresh water, a marvel that such could be found on these grand rocks jutting from the Pacific. Floreana Island was a favorite spot, a cave in Asilo de la Paz provided respite from the sun and located nearby, a freshwater spring quenched our thirst as no bottle of rum or cup of grog could. The many splendid coves sheltered my beloved ship and I put these islands on our map as a refuge to revisit. A pirate's paradise.

Humans in submersibles are a particular delight for me. I toy with them, terrorizing them, before sending them to rest forevermore in Davey Jones' Locker. He, the true devil of the sea, not I, though I have been called that at times—and deservedly so—while still a captain of the high seas.

I had heard the tales of a red shadow. And I have seen it, this entity, while swimming the coastal inlets of the Pacific, shores engulfed by wildfires that clawed as red fingers, like lava flows, at the slopes of distant mountains. A vaporous figure, barely discernible, scintillating the colors of fire, moving slowly among the towering torches, a great cloak of trailing flame. Stopping to admire the most radiant of embers, as one would wildflowers. And standing, arms outstretched, within a wall of thundering flame, as though it were a waterfall.

Time is a funny thing. And I have much time. Time to think. Too much thinking. And the more I think, the less anything really makes any sense to me. When I concentrate on a word long enough, saying it over and over, it begins to lose all meaning. It does not gain more. I do not gain some special insight. Rather, it simply becomes nonsense. I often wonder why that is. Why is meaning ephemeral? That to concentrate on meaning, it dissipates, like a sea fog before the sun? But I have learned. I know now. Meaning is what you make it. And what you make of it.

I have seen the apparitions of drowned sailors a league deep in the open ocean. They move along the currents, like jellyfish, translucent and hollowed out. Drifting. An obscured evaporation of life, grainy recordings seen through a mist ringing the eyes. Their netherworld interfaces with ours. I have no answer to their mystery.

I have spent time in the Devil's Triangle. Bermuda holds many fond memories for me. Barrels of rum and more booty than one can easily imagine. I have found no indication of paranormal activity, neither then nor now. However, strange occurrences abound there. I have firsthand experience. I think it to be strange natural energies from the planet itself. Electromagnetic fields that wreak havoc on a ship's instrumentation and cause various hallucinations through its action upon the human mind. Modern science, in which I hold much faith, shows this to be so in connection with such. I vastly enjoy a good ghost story, but I can ascribe none to this very odd place. Though I would heartily like to do so.

I have, however, found what I believe to be the sunken city of Atlantis. I seek still the remnants of the lost continent of Lemuria, an irrational search for it is a discredited theory. I have found evidence of other great civilizations, rivaling Atlantis, neither conjectured of nor even hinted at by mankind. Civilizations that long preceded our own and have been obliterated by the ravages of time. I have found technologies long since ensconced in sedimentary rock that speak to these previous iterations of highly advanced human civilizations. I can only surmise as to the great calamities that brought about their downfall.

Most astonishingly, I once discovered an alien ship, contained as though it were a fly in amber, at the bottommost extent of a glacier still graduating its way into the Southern Ocean, beneath which I swam. The salt water had polished the ice, creating a lens of sorts through which to view the artifact. It looked as though it were made of quicksilver. It was just beyond my ability to see its details clearly, though its shape was unmistakable. A saucer-like ship, similar to the other, reflecting a silver sheen through a great frozen veil. It raised many questions and disquieted my closest held sense of history. Intent upon documenting my discovery, I had returned, but the ship was gone, its coffin of ice having been torn asunder by the sea.

I have gathered, like the mysterious Captain Nemo, great quantities of bullion from the wrecks of Spanish galleons. For I can go where none are easily able, unhindered by ordinary constraints. I have found some by chance, some by memory, and some through careful research and expedition. I have meditated upon the good that gold can do. And the evil. It is an otherworldly substance, its properties unique and its value comprehended as being more than that assigned to it by man. It has a preternatural beauty. Sunshine. In solid form. Sunlight. Made tangible. The product of a strange and cosmic alchemy. One that exerts an influence over our minds that goes beyond the fevered lust that it incites in us for the extravagances of wealth that it permits. Rather, its power lies in the world of our dreams. Dreams caught. Dreams woven. Dreams made. Gold the dream maker. The dream manifester. My vast riches are regularly supplemented by this most enjoyable of hobbies—the retrieval of bullion long lost. It is a tranquility.

I have felt the remote age of the universe in the wind, sensed its steady expansion like the turning hands of a clock, felt its limitless and alien expanse in the warmth of the sun, sensed the flashing temporality of life in the rocky geology upon which I stood. The feeling was that of an endless plain in the gloaming. Millennia falling away like the petals of an old flower.

I have heard the susurrus of high-energy particles torrenting through the atmosphere. Have felt the atoms dancing on my skin, detected them teeming in the air about me, an evaporative and all-encompassing cloud of specks moving just beyond routine perception. We are awash in atoms. A cosmic ocean of atoms from which a cohort is drawn together into a discrete form, traveling a unique energy pathway for the briefest moment in time, then dispersing, flowing back into the ocean atomic, star travelers, flotsam among the galaxies.

A physical universe is a stark place. Cold to the soul. The only insulation being the beliefs in which we wrap ourselves. In these moments I have felt a sense of profound isolation. And sadness. Maybe that will change, but I did not feel a sense of tranquility and oneness. I did not feel a sense of spirituality connecting me to some grand and purposeful cosmic architecture of harmonic energies and celestial vibrations. I just felt strange, an incoherence of being, empty inside. A hollow kite far aloft, through which the ceaseless winds of time blew.

This opening up to the infinite and indifferent scale of the universe has not been the catalyst for some great spiritual epiphany. Rather, it has been dismal. And deeply unsettling. It is only something that I have experienced because I have time, so much time. It was not precipitated by mindfulness or meditation, just idle time. In the frenetic dealings of a mortal life, one has so little time. The mad race consumes us, our every waking moment, and jars us from the sanctuary of our slumber.

The sound of the sea was almost soothing in these moments. These moods. And I often went to it. But it fell short of being so. For it was also hollow. A sound disconnected and untethered. Scattered frequencies tumbling through the wind. And I felt separate from it, removed, perhaps even a sense of having turned away, a cherished and long distant home that I could never return to in innocence.

I think that I now better understand why mortals cling to one another pathologically, madly, feverishly, why they numb their senses with intoxicants and cloud themselves with mindless entertainment. It is an illusion of solace. And they feel it to be so. It is flimsy, false, and fleeting. An artifice. If you aren't at peace with your place in the universe and with what the universe is, then there is no solace to be had. Maybe that's the spiritual part, I don't know. I don't pretend to know. I'll leave that to the charlatans. And to those very few who actually do.

Madness comes easily enough. Washing over me like the waves of the North Sea. But I regain my buoyancy, always through sheer force of will, the blazing light of which drives the deep and ever-grasping shadows to a thwarted distance. Though my dark transformation brought about many things, an immunity of the psyche and of the soul was not one of them. Even I, the Captain General of the Sea—il Capitano Generale da Mar, was not invulnerable to the tempests of my own nature. But given enough time and singular focus, perhaps I could become so. And perhaps, perhaps God will present itself in a form that I can recognize. For I know it to be possible that what I have just described to you is in fact God presenting itself to me. Who am I to impose my expectations on that experience?

And so. Experiences. At times, I reflect upon my condition and gain some measure of appreciation for the experiences it allows me. Experiences far beyond the ken of mortals. The thresholds of the physical being do not limit me in comparison. I am able to comfortably withstand what would surely kill mortals in an instant. Nor am I limited by a need for sleep. And though I hunger and thirst, it is more driven by a desire and an instinct to kill than by the actual need for nourishment to sustain my physical being and my efforts. But that is while the moon is full. My weakness besets me before and after my three days of havoc are wreaked upon the world each month, for that is when I become almost like you. Almost mortal. It is when I am weak that I wish to be something other than I am. But during the glorious hysteria of my transformation, I revel in my powers. Which have heightened greatly since my inception. And they will continue to. I am most curious to see the extent to which they do. And as mentioned, I relish the thought of vanquishing my older colleagues who share in this condition. I feel this way even when not in a state of transformation. Mayhap I have always had a twist of the evil in me. Perhaps this is why I was chosen. Or I have become so. I do not rightly know. My long meditations on this matter over the years have led me no closer to the truth of my spiritual substance than I was five-hundred years ago. Knowledge of my true being is an elusive and hard sought prize. I had journeyed to Nepal, and later Tibet, hoping to find my truth of essence through the isolation of Buddhist practice. I envisioned finding enlightenment in a monastery high in the Himalayas. But the distance from the sea soon proved a profound impracticality and I have not returned since. I had endeavored to bring a monk to California to further my practice in meditation, but word of what I was had spread, seemingly telepathically, among the communities there and none would accept my proposition. I would not hire any but them. And so it is. Even the greatest of wealth cannot buy everything as it turns out. Interesting—and as it should be—that it is in the realm of the spiritual that the buck does indeed stop. Crooked pastors notwithstanding.

I have pushed myself to the extreme, to the very limits in my transformation and managed to swim farther and faster than I had ever imagined possible. Always at the back of mind is that I might encounter one of the elders. It will happen eventually. I have rehearsed time and again my actions in that situation. A bold and decisive attack is the best strategy and the only real option. I push myself to quicken the process of my strengthening. I have noticed that while maturation through age amplifies and grows my powers, so too does the physical stress with which I subject myself. I am in training therefore, to dispose of those whom I know would wish to do the same with me—and think nothing of it. Long ago, I had met my elders by chance, one soon after the other as fate would have it. I escaped with my life but only narrowly. Elements had been in my favor both times, an advantage that allowed for the slimmest margins of escape. Their power was formidable, but I also sensed that neither would have been my match before our respective inception. This translation of both natural and battle-won abilities helped my cause in those moments, if only slightly. My survival was measured in milliseconds and millimeters. I swore that upon our next meeting, the tables would be reversed and victory would be mine. I have since escalated my aspiration from that of mere victory to their demise. I will not look over my shoulder for a thousand years. Then another. I will not fear the attack of a most dangerous and sophisticated enemy. Rather, it will be I who attacks. If by ambush, sobeit. I have focused my mind on this course of action and my resolve in the matter has crystallized. Forming a geological intent. The accretion of my thoughts as real as any stone dagger in the hand, chiseled by time, burnished with anticipation and fired hard and sinister by a dark desire. I will have my blood.

Only the creatures of the great marine know that sunlight will make two parts of the same sea a blue and a green and when they mix, a kaleidoscope of color bursts forth beneath the waves. I have seen saltwater sizzle with golden sheets of sunlight, effervescing yellow bubbles into a bluebright, refracting air. I stay as deep as necessary to avoid direct contact with sunlight, but although such would be painful, it would not be deadly for me. I am, after all, no vampire. And make no mistake, there are vampires of the sea. I have beheld them. They live in the wreckage of sunken ships and prey on scuba divers and cruise ship passengers. They are an especially unpleasant lot and prone to cruel fits of a waterborne melancholy, lamenting a long distant and preferred life on land. I have not yet been able to ascertain how they found themselves to be in their present circumstances. They are most unfriendly and not at all receptive to conversation. And so,

I can only conjecture. Another mystery for my book of mysteries. It has been said that the great underwater explorer Jacques Cousteau once encountered members of this disagreeable race, retiring soon thereafter. I know not if there is any truth to the story.

I have often pursued my fascination with the bizarre realm of fungi. The Roman god of fungi, Robigus, was greatly revered and feared. And most rightly so. That a mushroom is the flower of a fungus residing deep beneath the surface of the soil, sending up a long filament to the light, that they are classified as being neither plant nor animal, has sparked a great and enduring curiosity within me. They possess a chemical intelligence, a chemical communication transmitted through vast, subterranean territories. A deep kingdom of the darkest chambers. A labyrinth of fungal intelligence. Fungi can make zombies of wasps and other creatures, controlling their very behavior. They are a strange and alien life form. Look no further for otherworldly intelligences, we share our own with many. I have wondered if perhaps a luciferin and luciferase producing fungus or alga is the reason for the ever-intensifying bioluminescence of my race? (Ah! There he is again. Lucifer. The light-bringer.) Alga means seaweed in Latin, and I am brought back to the sea, always back to the sea. I once dug down 35 feet below the forest floor in the wilderness of Oregon to get at the fungus from which the mushroom flowered. I sensed it to be hostile to my efforts, like unearthing some pale and dangerous insect just beneath the soil of a rock, a presence better left hidden by its own dark devices. A gray and misshapen, fleshy mass, insinuated throughout the soil, an alien brain, pulsing malevolence. I smelled its sinister intelligence, a chemical signature that left my heightened olfactory sense smarting for days after. I have done battle with the hissing Yateveo plant of South America, the Devil's Snare of Central America and the Madagascar tree among others, but while their aggression was of a seemingly automatic and purely physical nature, like that of the Venus flytrap, this presented an insidious and pervading atmosphere of hostile intent. A telepathic malice manifested by a keen and formidable intelligence. Perhaps the product of the combined forces of fungal networks and colonies that stretch for miles, silent and mostly unseen, deep below our feet, as has been found. I cannot be entirely sure if the organism was inherently evil, or simply employing a strategy of deterrence—ultimately justified, though I meant it no real harm—intended to thwart the invasion of its underground domain. I am, however, inclined to believe the former. That fungi do not rely upon chlorophyll to conduct photosynthesis for survival leads me to question their origins. That various mushrooms also contain powerful hallucinogens and poisons has further fueled my curiosity concerning this strange life form. They are able to manipulate our perceptions and to kill. They are chemists. Dependent upon neither the light of the sun nor moonglow. I no longer consume mushrooms. Perhaps there will come a day when there will be more things in this world that I avoid than those that I do not. Only time will tell.

As I have told you, in my human form, I eschew all forms of meat, whether from on land or from in sea. I had begun as a vegan, but unable to abstain from enjoying the many delights of dairy I am now simply a vegetarian, but that is the extent of my direct culinary interaction with animal products. I have at times bought out the entirety of the lobsters crawling about restaurant aquariums, rubber bands on their claws, to release them into the sea. This amuses me. I am perhaps the patron saint of the lobster. A strange creature that is quite delicious despite some of its more unsavory insectoid aspects. I have consumed many the line of marching lobsters during my time in transformation, my jaws appreciating the exercise, like chewing gum when I am bored during my dryland sojourns. But when human, I am repulsed by the idea of consuming creatures of the sea and land. A surf and turf restaurant is the most abhorrent of places to me now. Long before all of this though, I loved such eateries. In Italy, I recall a little cafe near Rome, but closer to the sea, that served an exquisite crab carbonara. I shudder now to think of the dish. Frustrated with the readily available and mass-produced offerings for vegetarians, I invested in creating my own line of ready-made, vegetarian cuisine. I am very happy with it and it is selling very well. Wealth begets more wealth, but I donate all profits to charitable organizations, à la Newman's Own, especially those that protect the sea from the ravages of human civilization.

I once desired a career in film. I had the time. Why not the fame and the lark? I laugh now. What a repugnant and odious industry. Hedonistic hypocrites of the highest order. Miscreants, perverts, and drug addled ne'er do wells who desperately crave the attention of others. Pathetic. I soon learned the error of that ambition. I am many things, but I am not suited to the life of an actor. In my days at sea I would have run such unholy fiends through with my cutlass. The Romans buried actors in separate cemeteries, no sign of respect and a sensibility that I now understand fully. And I have done long and frequent battle with Roman galleys and hold nothing but the utmost respect for that great and warring race of man. If not a Hibernian, I would have most desired to be a Roman.

I thirst for the most dire of consequences for aberrant behavior. In my time as a sea captain, absolute order was upheld through the gravest of punishments. Though I were a pirate, aboard my ship, absolute order ruled. The rule of my law was absolute. One knew what one would get if the rules were broken, if our code of conduct was not adhered to. All were content as all knew the consequences for their actions. No leniency was given. No excuses accepted. No justifications made. No exploitations of loopholes. No variation and no negotiation. There was no agenda but quick justice. I see a society now that would benefit greatly from the same enforcement of laws as that aboard a pirate ship. I see endless excuses and finger pointing, deflection and redirection, a lack of personal responsibility, misguided justifications, rationalizations, and appeasement and the enabling of more of the same. I see relativistic arguments and worldviews, as corrosive as any acid to the framework of society, such that objective and universal truths, standards and the norms of human conduct will eventually cease to exist if we continue on this course. I see an erosion in values and ethics and a wholesale destruction of the collective moral compass. I see the criminal painted as the victim and the victim stripped of their justice. None of that would be allowed on a pirate ship. Consequences are meted out for actions done. Period. Are you surprised to hear a once-feared pirate speak like this? You shouldn't be. We may have been wolves of the high sea, but we abided strictly by a code of conduct that was enforced with ruthless and lethal efficiency. An eye for an eye leaves the whole world blind some would say. What utter rubbish I say! If the actions warrant it, sobeit, for without it, an attitude of indifference and disobedience develops, creeping in bit by bit like a vile mold and eventually devouring law and order, putrefying it, hollowing it out and rendering it worthless. Replacing consequences for one's actions with falsities, warped platitudes, disingenuous apologies, and no actual contrition is the road to society's ruin, just as it would be on any pirate ship of old. There was a time that a thief's hand was cut off for stealing. Now the thief is made to be the victim and the baker the criminal. Unconscionable! And unfathomable in its gross stupidity. Do not throw pearl before swine. Nothing works better to keep the human animal in line than fear and retribution. On my ship, fear made my men lawful. Lawlessness was not given the chance to be emboldened and to fester. It was stamped out like a hissing cockroach. As such, we were highly efficient in our endeavors for no clouds of doubt hung about the ship. No gray. Just black and white. Much like the Jolly Roger itself. I hold to the severest of punishments and discipline for those who choose to break the laws. It has served me well and I would have it no other way. Society would do well to adopt the same approach. But I am not a man of this day and age. And so, I remain baffled. But what of my own great lawlessness, you may ask? Aye, if I were to have been caught, I would have accepted my fate and the consequences of my deeds. I would not have asked for forgiveness nor lenience. I would not have blamed my transformation. I chose my path of blood and plunder—no other.

When I am deep in my cups and memories flow like wine from my mind to my heart as from the bottle to the chalice, I feel again the embrace of my wife, though centuries removed, as if it were only moments ago. Time is a fleeting stag, a blurred and distant vapor before unfocused eyes. Time is neither friend nor foe. But it can be made either. It is of your choosing. I once made it my enemy. But no longer. And time has forgiven me my foolishness. It is the only friend I have now, save Blackbeard.

Ah, Blackbeard. I think him to be a loyal friend but I cannot be sure. Perhaps he entertains the same notions towards me that I entertain towards the elder ones. Perhaps he harbors a thousand, clawing hatreds of me for changing him. It takes years long to come to terms with one's transformation into a wereshark. Perhaps someday he will attempt my assassination. And perhaps he will prevail. Until then, we shall drink together as only sailors of the high seas can, pirates we, those who have done many a long battle shoulder to bloody shoulder, back to bloody back.

And here we come to the part of my memoir that is most unexpected. It was for me the equivalent of wandering out of Plato's cave and seeing the world for what it really was. No more shadows. I had always believed that my transformation had been wrought by a confluence of natural elements and strange energies on the night of my change on that serene beach in Sicily. Some strange alchemy. An interaction born of pure and extraordinary chance. I remembered nothing of it and as I awoke on the shores of a distant land, profoundly confused but otherwise unscathed, and as I did not yet understand what I had become, the thought that a creature of the night sea and the full moon had done this to me had not entered my mind. Not then, and not even much later. Rather, the truth was delivered to me as lightning in the night.

You can imagine my surprise when I learned the truth. The truth of my origin. Read on, sweet soul, as my life's tale nears its completion to the here and now.

There is a third elder. The one that changed me. I did not learn of her existence until quite recently. Her age and power are beyond reckoning. I would stand no chance in battle against her, but neither do I desire to do so. I met her in the open ocean, somewhere between Madagascar and Australia. It was not a chance encounter. She had finally decided to introduce herself to me. Perhaps judging me to be ready for such, to have matured. My anguishes blunted by time. And she was kind. Benevolent. It was most unexpected. The others I had met were instantly hostile, cruel and aggressive, intent upon killing me. This elder was almost motherly. She has progressed to a permanent state of transformation, unaffected by the full moon, the light of the sun, saltwater or freshwater, or even the need for carnage. She lives as any shark might. No more, no less, really, but for the exceptional intelligence of a human who has seen the rise of civilization itself. She swam the Tigris and Euphrates, watched as Mesopotamia brought writing and the ziggurats into being and saw the flourishing of Babylon. She swam the Mediterranean and the Nile as the great pyramids were built and the Phoenicians sailed and the ancient Greeks constructed their temples and Alexandria shone its light across the sea and the Roman empire spread throughout the known world and Jesus walked the Holy Land. She swam the waters of the Indus as civilization grew and China rose and the Americas embraced the stars and the zero. She swam the coasts as Stonehenge and the mo'ai proclaimed their silhouette, as coral reefs began their dance of stone and redwoods green-wove the air in a lattice to the sun. She has read and learned more than any other soul in history. She is a great library of knowledge and of vast experience. And she told me of my change. She had just happened to spy me on the Sicilian shore on that fateful night. The light of the full moon glinting off my bottle of cognac. Smoke from my pipe dancing as phantoms in the gentle breeze. And she had desired to make another like herself. Call it selfishness, or loneliness, or boredom even, she could not be sure. She had created the other two elders as well. She knew of Blackbeard and was certain that I alone had created another. The other elders would not, as they saw any other as their sworn enemy. Even her. She avoids them, only to spare their most swift and assured death. I found it hard to hear—the details of my transformation—but was not upset with her. It was done and I had become what I had become and there she was. Another of my kind from whom I could learn so much and with whom I could perhaps find friendship. Even a deep and abiding kinship. I told her of my plan to eliminate the two elders and she did not dissuade me. It seemed that she may have even thought it to be a good idea, but had no desire for doing so herself. We talked of the possibility of creating others who could also share in a lasting friendship and in the Seven Seas. The possibility of creating a small community of our race. Of sharing the many thousands of years to come together instead of being apart, alone, isolated. It warmed my thoughts to speak of such.

We will see what transpires. I have become quite cynical over the years. But I resolutely hope for the best. I would like such a community. A sense of belonging and comradeship would make being what I am so much more bearable. Regularly seeing others such as I would be a salve for my soul. Do I dare to hope? Yes. Yes, I dare to. I think that I shall permit myself this greatest and most meaningful of luxuries. Yes. I am resolved in the matter. I shall allow myself to hope once more.

I am a wereshark. This is my story.

PART II

~ III ~

FRANKENSTEIN'S MONSTER

Dear reader, hello, again. I had left you previously with that bold statement of my hope for the future in the first telling of this now greatly expanded record of my stories, my memoir. For those of you reading this just now, that statement of hope will be much fresher in your minds. I will keep this short as it is not something that I choose to dwell upon and requires but a mention as I have grown beyond it—and so the retelling is of little interest to me anyway. But you should know what happened. I owe you that much, dear reader. As you may recall, I had believed that with the eldest wereshark and perhaps Blackbeard too, that we would be able to create a community of our own. The idea of a thing can seem to be the very essence of perfection. A bright flower of the mind. Vibrant and unsurpassed in its beauty. We believe in its possibilities, that it is feasible to implement and will be sustainable. However, sometimes the idea is flawed and impractical, with the process more complicated and presenting more difficulties and challenges than was expected. The idea turns out to be a hothouse flower, elegant perhaps, but little suited to survival beyond the glass. One may soldier on for a bit, until finally relinquishing the idea entirely, setting it free to fly far and distant overhead, fading like the faint exclamation of wild geese into the eternal blue. It is simply the way of things. Regrettably. Reality is a world apart from our ideas and our ideals. Blackbeard, though a good friend still, simply did not share in this utopic vision of weresharks, having little interest in such and being far too busy with his own ventures. He never fully committed to the effort and contributed little. Eventually removing himself from the process entirely. I hold no hard feelings in the matter. The eldest was kind and wise and patient, but in the end, not suited for our little experiment in society building. It required a level of planning and organization, a structuring of one's life and activities and thoughts in a manner that chafed greatly at her sensibilities and acted as a damper upon her boundless and free-spirited approach to existence. She lived to explore. Each day a new adventure. She was enormously wise and learned yet she lacked the discipline to make manifest in the physical world the idea with which we had both seemingly been so enamored. After her initial burst of inspiration had been spent, she gradually became bored with it all, withdrawing her energies bit by bit, until finally when she had lost all interest in the effort, she simply swam away and I have not seen her since. I cannot blame her. She is a bondless creature, more an entity really, and the details of governance are monotonous and governance itself imposes strictures on all those encompassed by it. Perhaps we had overreached with the scale of our vision and should have first tried to form a very loose association and if that was sustainable, to have slowly built the structures of our society and then to have gradually increased the population of our brethren—and this was another most challenging issue to be dealt with as we had no way of knowing if someone would transform as I had or Blackbeard or instead would transform as the other two younger elders had. And we would need to guide them and teach them and in truth, none of us had the desire to do that, nor the patience. And that was that. The fever dream resolved itself. And here I am. Nothing has changed. I drink more rum and red wine than any three men could—or should. I write my memoir and undertake my various adventures. I smoke my pipe and laugh at the warning labels on the bags of tobacco; warnings appear on everything, put there by the catastrophizing mice of bureaucracy, squeaking with self-righteous importance in their comfortable offices as they steadily eat away at our freedoms in the name of what is good for us. Are we to thank them? I would sooner run them through with my cutlass! I still paint a little, but not very well—that has not changed either. I write some poetry, read some books and stir up very little mischief for the most part—at least around the stronghold, as my adventures far afield do tend to take on a life of their own.

Leaving the daily life of the sea has been the most difficult thing I have ever had to do. I did so because I needed to reinvent myself. I would not continue my pirating ways for untold years to come. I needed to find a new journey to immerse myself fully in for the next five-hundred years. And anyway, the pirating life had already begun to change in ways that were not to my liking as a traditionalist. I had grown to love pirating the way it was, had become one with how it had been. Further to this, I sensed that as an enterprise, it was waning into oblivion. I needed to find an entirely different undertaking, a fresh start, not a slow and forced transition into some new and diluted version of the original. And so, I took to dry land. Terra firma. It was not easy. And I had much to learn. I had at first gone far from the sea, but found that to be an agony, a condition of being to which I had gradually become accustomed to. I then routinely increased my distance from the sea, until it became almost comfortable. Finally, it had become so, and though I must return to the sea if at all possible when in transformation, I grew to barely miss it.

When walking the great forests, I am never alone. For I have my thoughts. And I have my memories. The luminosity of my black heart, mon coeur noir, paces me at a near distance, flickering darkly from between the trees. A reminder of what I have been but also of what I can one day be. Life on land is a slow healing of the long, deep scars of the sea.

I have found the frozen expanses of the North and South Poles to be wonderous realms of beauty and purity. Snow and ice, frigid winds and a pale sun do much in creating antiseptic conditions. I found it to be delightful and a pleasant respite from the near-constant jackhammering of odors that my olfactory sense is subjected to elsewhere. They say that a shark can smell blood from a mile away, I say it's more like two. I have explored vast ice caves that glowed sky blue and found extraordinary things beneath deep layers of snow and ice. I can say with all confidence that a great and highly advanced civilization once flourished in Antarctica while it was still a warm and verdant place. I have found no evidence though of a secret Nazi or UFO base under the snow nor have I found another alien ship in the ice, but that does not mean that I will not. I have come to understand that my perception of reality can change in the quickest of moments. I hold no subscriptions dear.

The strangest encounter that I have had in the northernmost reaches is with a creature well-known in popular culture; that being Frankenstein's monster itself. Not a work of fiction after all. He who fled atop an ice raft towards what was thought to be a most certain death, even for an entity of such remarkable physique and constitution. I smelled him long before I saw or heard him. A horrid stench. For a moment I thought it might be a polar bear. And when I first laid eyes upon the creature, I still thought the same, but only for a moment. For here was a marvel indeed. A gargantuan, man-like creature the size of any polar bear and wearing the furs of those very same animals such that he looked for all the world to be one himself. Or more so, the Yeti, but I knew this was not its haunt. A great wall of white moving quickly towards me. He approached with a dangerous urgency and as I was not yet in a state of transformation, his presence could be found lethal. Having read the book, I knew that he could not be trusted, no matter how miserable and tragic his fate may have been. He alone having chosen the grand design of the terror and death he inflicted upon his victims. I know of that which I speak. And I am ruthlessly adept at seeing through subterfuge and self-serving delusion. In truth, I am most masterfully expert in this regard. I could sense the evil energies roiling about him as though vibrations emanating from the infernal engines of evil that animated the creature and propelled it on its wicked course. His sinister aura was visible to my eye much as a heat mirage would be, a twilight silver shimmer contrasting rather clearly with the surrounding snow. And my eyes saw the cunning in his own. A true deviant most foul. So many dark facets of the soul contained in a creature that may have lacked one altogether. But I cannot be the judge of that, it is of a realm beyond my ken. He at first attempted to charm my suspicions away with mead-like talk, surmising that I was no fool and desiring the various accoutrements with which I was well equipped and from which he would have liked to separate me, we spoke for a time, days perhaps. There were, however, many things that he could not know. I reckoned my age to be hundreds of years beyond his own and also knew that my powers far exceeded his, but not at this moment. My ability to out-think an opponent is a witchcraft, a wizardry born of long years and intense development of the mind and the indirect amplification of its properties in the unknown territories of that sphere. Being near to the water I knew that if I could delay his inevitable attack for just a while longer, I would be able to escape his dark designs. And so, providing a pretense of ever-greatening interest in the creature and in asking many questions, I was able to prolong our conversation with a renewed energy until the full moon shone like a silver sun across the Great White North and I felt the transformation begin. Perhaps I had underestimated the depths of the creature's cunning, of its own wizardry of the mind for it had made a quick and precise calculus; the fiend seemed to understand what was at hand and lunged towards me in a flashing avalanche of white fur and gnashing yellow teeth. Had I not been somewhat empowered by the transformation underway, I would not have been able to elude his deadly-quick grasp. The creature spun as a ballerina might, an almost comical sight, light and nimble on his feet, a far faster and more agile adversary than any I had yet met, save the elders of my own kind and also no more so than the Yeti and the Sasquatch, both of whom I have had terrible and incomprehensibly violent battles with—but I digress, as those are stories for another time. The realization that I had underestimated my foe sent a burst of adrenaline coursing through my veins. I pivoted, punching the creature with all of my might, my fist disappearing into untold layers of polar bear skins.

He howled loudly, though I knew that it was more in great irritation than pain. I was still far from fully transformed. I needed to get away from this beast and to the water if I were to win this battle. Despite the dire situation unfolding, I was having a bit of fun indeed. Not unlike the old days, with Blackbeard by my side, as we went over the gunwales into the fray of bloody-blessed battle. I roared with laughter and ran for my life towards the sea, that massive white devil close on my heels by the sound of it. I raced across the snow like an Arctic hare, only sinking in deeply from time to time, while the hulking creature, now farther and farther behind me found it to be much slower going indeed. I dove into a great and undulating fracture in the ice and hit the water in mid-transformation. The cold much more of a shock than it would have otherwise been, but as my transformation progressed, I became increasingly comfortable with the temperature of the water, swimming through the mazes of fractures and celebrating my escape. Upon full transformation, I sunk just below the surface and waited, much like a crocodile, for my prey to present itself. I did not have long to wait. The creature came like an enraged silverback thrashing across the ice, bellowing Victorian-era challenges and demanding that I should show myself. I grinned. Ah, but anger makes a fool of us all. His wrath would be his undoing. He simply need stay off the ice and away from the sea. But he would do neither. I swam downwards a length, then turning sped upwards through the water as though a dorsal-finned torpedo. I breached the surface and rightly, I flew. The creature turned in time to see his toothy-grinned doom fast approaching. A pale demon of the deep, hurtling through the air like a great spear in the bright light of the moon. My impact was a detonation, hitting him with such a tremendous force that I drove him into the sea like a ragdoll. Whereupon I tore into him layer by layer, unwrapping my gift of blood to the bone, descending into the depths as those very layers floated serenely upwards, until the creature was little more than a spine and its skull, like a bell on a chord, soon to rest on the sea floor forevermore. So ended Frankenstein's monster these many years after its supposed demise. That tragic tale now truly told and finished. The world free of its lurking and self-indulgent evil at great last.

~ IV ~

THE MONK SORCERER

I have regaled you with my tales both slow and quick throughout this memoir, with the truth of my lived experience the thread that connects them as the fabric of any garment, this of the memory. Here is another. Long ago, while still obsessed with the attainment of wealth and social status, I had decided that I would become a baron or perhaps a viscount. Reasoning that my riches and notoriety would gain me entrée into the lower ranks of nobility, but into the ranks of nobility, nonetheless. No mean feat for one with my occupational pedigree. And I was right. Soon assuming the barony of a destitute nobleman in the easternmost reaches of Europe. With the title of nobility rightly transferred and the lucre exchanged, I gained possession of an ancient, vast and wildly overgrown estate with a badly dilapidated castle crumbling into ruin and into what had once been a moat now serving as a reeking, squealing swinery. No sooner was the old baron happily down the road, off to live luxuriously in Paris, then I set to work hiring crews of laborers from the countryside to rehabilitate the structures and the grounds. I had in mind what it should be once again and no amount of disrepair would stop me—or anything else for that matter. Or so I thought. On my first night in the castle, I knew that more was afoot than one would have initially and routinely noticed. For this discovery required staying the night. And in the deep of that night, I was awoken by the fluttering of odd nightbirds, they of a metallic purple black, flying in through the many broken stained-glass windows. I thought nothing of it at first. Why should I have? The next night, I was awoken again. This time by a faint whisper. I could not locate its origin, it seemed to be an almost ambient sound, pervading the space about me. But from where or from what it issued I did not know. On the third night, the whisper became a guttural, almost throaty broadcast and more pronounced. And by the fourth, it was a nearly palpable sound that swirled about the room. By this point, my concern in the matter had also become more pronounced as you may imagine. I was much too far from the sea and wondered what I had gotten myself into. By the fifth night, I began to comprehend a shape manifesting itself in the sound, a barely visible silhouette, dissolving and reforming like a dark cloud in the wind, over and over again. By the sixth night, the silhouette displayed more density of form, but would erratically change in both shape and consistency, reverting again to its slowly clarifying silhouette. It was at this point that I decided to change rooms but would return at night to spy on this one. That did not go to plan, as on the seventh night the silhouette appeared most clearly in my new quarters, accompanied by a sustained growl that rattled my wine glass from the night table and reverberated deeply through the myriad windows, causing several squares of stained glass to topple from their frames, exploding in flashes of muted color upon the stone floor below. I summoned my courage and called out a booming halt and a challenge to this strange presence, this force unknown, this entity of ominous intent. The response was not what I had hoped for. The growl only intensified and the silhouette grew darker, stormier, far larger and more resolute in its form and stature. I began to discern a cloaked figure, tall and pale and wicked, coming haltingly into focus, but only for the briefest of moments, to then shimmer and become nebulous once more. I had seen and heard enough. I bolted for the great oaken door that opened into the long hall and sprinted along it as only a man, immortal or not, can run believing the devil himself close upon his heels. I made for the stable, bridled my prize stallion, slung the bag of money, clothing, boots and pistols across my shoulder that I kept there for just such occasions—pirating had taught me much—and set off bareback, barefoot and pajama clad at a full gallop into the cold night in what I believed to be the general direction of the distant sea. I was not pursued. By daylight, though exhausted, I felt my courage rising once more but chose not to return to the castle. It was too removed from the sea for my liking anyway (though in my later years, it would not have been far enough), and

I was a baron still. I eventually made my way to Paris, and finding the old baron, asked him what he knew of the strange apparition that had haunted me from the first night of my stay. He told me a long and chilling tale of a monk and his descent into madness and evil who had once lived in a monastery not far from the castle during the days of Vlad the Impaler and who had become a fearsome sorcerer, a practitioner of the very blackest of the dark arts, upon having found a moldy book of evil incantations and rituals in a cave high in the mountains. That book most foul took grip upon his soul like a loathsome leach, draining it of the light. Only to be filled again with darkness. He had aided Vlad in his many battles against the invading Turks and later, desiring both the worldly and supernatural powers that Vlad held, turned on his steadfast ally and was vanquished. Since that time, his vengeful spirit had been a haunting on the countryside. The old baron stated that he had not once been bothered by the entity and was never sure why. But he surmised that I had been tormented immediately by it because I possessed some power that had offended it, reminding it of Vlad's own much-vaunted powers. How very right he was, without even knowing. Never to return, I later sold the estate but kept my title of nobility. And much later, I used those very same legal and heraldic papers to light a fire most regal upon my hearth, caring nothing for their value. Perhaps you thought that I would have encountered Dracula himself while there? I would have thought so too, but such was not to be. I can only conjecture that the Prince of Darkness prefers the blood of regular folk to that of a bioluminescent wereshark with old sea brine and rum for blood.

the flames of darkness and we, the blood of creation, milk
to float the Elohim in serene creation; with God set before
and him for blood.

~ V ~

THE YETI

Around the time I had decided that I should try in earnest to find my spiritual self in a monastery with the Buddhist monks, I had been mountaineering in Nepal and Tibet and the Hindu Kush. It was here that I first came upon the infamous Yeti. But unlike the experience of Tintin during his sojourn in Tibet, I had gone in search of the great white beast. In a sense, I had become a dryland Captain Ahab, having become utterly obsessed not only with the notion of the Yeti but of the Sasquatch of the Great Pacific Northwest and environs and of all of the many variations of these creatures that are spoken of throughout the world. The idea of spying one of these creatures positively thrilled my soul with a wild electricity. My first and only encounter was of such exceptional violence and mayhem that I still grin wide then wince a little when remembering the event that unfolded. I had left a small village late in the day, hiking farther into the remote and dizzying reaches of Nepal. The fading sun glowed gently from the snow and placed halos around the mountaintops, an almost mystical vision of the beauty and grandeur and magnificence and false tranquility of the natural world—for this is a glorious façade, an ornate and mesmerizing sheath within which the cold steel of quick death bides its time in anticipation of the missteps of the foolish and unwary, those easily lulled by its beauty, the sublime beauty of nature, who forget that such beauty is no insulation from its raw brutality, the sheer lethality of the natural world. It will kill you the moment you become distracted, the moment you have become too comfortable in its parlor. That you can rest assured. Have you not experienced this yourself? I think that you have and thus you understand that of which I speak. If you are reading this now, then not the death clearly, you escaped—bravo!—but barely, and you knew then as you know now just how close it is that you have come to meeting your maker. Raise your glass high and sip well from the sweet chalice of life a bit longer. As the sun set pale and the white moon rose, the snow sparkled like great fields of diamonds around me. Earlier that day, I had learned from villagers that an ice cave existed some miles into the mountains and I had determined that I would find it that night. The mountainous terrain was as rugged a place I'd traveled and I took great care in my expedition. Once almost slipping into a crevasse that opened black and yawning from beneath a sheet of sliding snow. As I ventured deeper into the mountains, I would sense from time to time that I was being watched. An unsettling feeling and one that kept me alert and mindful of the many dangers. On several occasions I detected motion in my peripheral vision, but each time when I quickly turned to look, I saw nothing but the snow on the sides of the mountains. But I knew something was there, though exactly what remained to be seen. I was on the alert. They say that even paranoids are right some of the time. This is a truth. One that I had learned from centuries of battles anticipated, battles fought and battles reflected upon. I paid heed to my instincts. It had saved my skin more times than I could remember. Eventually, I came to a great chasm interrupting my march through the endless succession of mountains. I stood close by its edge, looking down into the faintly lit feature, disappearing into blackness. I could hear but not see that a frigid river of meltwater flowed robustly far below. My mind so absorbed, I momentarily dropped my guard. It was then that the attack came, in a blinding explosion of pain, shooting stars and undesired levitation. My stealthy adversary had watched and waited patiently, biding its time most admirably, until having sensed my preoccupation, it had struck in an inspired flash of enthusiastic violence. I could hardly believe what was happening and cursed myself for having been caught off guard. It was unlike me and very few creatures were capable of doing such, this then, was a wily and most dangerous opponent. These thoughts were instantaneously replaced by the realization that I was now hurtling headlong into said chasm, flailing and twisting and spinning like a dandelion seed riding the wind. Within moments I had hit the water. The impact was forceful, like a sledgehammer to my chest, but I had somehow been lucky enough to have plunged into the deep of it, clear of the rocks. But the cold of it felt like a beating from clubs. It shuddered me and knocked the air out of my lungs. I gasped for air and struggled to remain afloat and conscious as the swift water carried me down the mountain, eventually depositing me into a lake with a tiny island of rocks situated therein. I swam in utter exhaustion with the fading push of the river's flow towards it, being able to reason through the fog of my mind that it might offer me some safety from the prowling Yeti. I did not know if it had followed along with me from above or might soon find me and set out to finish its work. Only that it was not the dead of winter and that I had some innate fortitude as a wereshark though not in transformation, did I not perish that night from the impact of my fall nor of hypothermia. I dragged myself unto the little island and found shelter between the rocks. Falling unconscious a moment later. I stayed so for how long I do not know, but when I awoke the sun was shining high in a sharp-blue sky. I was numb with cold and fatigue and weak from hunger and thirst. My body ached all over. I managed to hoist myself up and took ponderous steps to drink from the lake. The water refreshed my strength a little. I staggered about my island of stones and found fresh-water mussels layering the rocky pools along with cold-water algae, and I spied the silvery glint of darting mountain trout. So, there would be food, though the trout might be safe from me for the time being. I gorged myself on a large population of the island's mussels, then used their shells to scrape algae from the rocks, making a nice salad as it were. I had no qualms about suddenly having fallen off the veggie wagon as this was a matter of immediate survival—I did not have the luxury of it being otherwise. I dried my clothing and boots in the sun such as it was, drank more water and began to feel revived. I surveyed my environs more closely now. The lake was a fairly large one, stretching a ways into the distance. I was near one end of it and more or less equidistant from its sides. It would make a good enough refuge for the time being as I gave some thought to my current predicament and set about putting together a plan of escape. Though I had neither seen nor heard the Yeti since it had hurled me off the cliff and headlong into the freezing-cold river far below, I reasoned that it must be lurking about some-where. After all, it had expertly shadowed me and with such a degree of sinister intent that I doubted it would stop until achieving its objective, that of my demise. How curious to be the stalked and the hunted. But the joke would be on my foe in the end, as it had no understand-ing of what it was dealing with. Understand too, dear reader, that by this time in my maturation and develop-ment as a wereshark, though I needed water when trans-formed—my one true weakness, it did not have to be saltwater. Freshwater would suffice. Saltwater is greatly preferred, of course, as it was a crucial element in my origination into this werecreature of the sea and is a part of my very being and of my very soul. But as long as

I have an aqueous environment in which to be when I am fully transformed, then I will be fine. That was not the case early on, as saltwater was necessary to my survival. My plan was an obvious one. I would wait until the full moon rose, transform in the lake, and kill my would-be predator with a most expressive joy in my heart. I grinned viciously, laughed out loud, hooted in joy and lay back for a cold nap in the pale sun of the Himalayas. Now, an important part of my plan involved agitating the Yeti over the coming days to such an extent that it would make its presence known to me immediately at the start of our interspecies sporting event. I wanted no surprises, but for those that I would most graciously bestow. I am a kind soul, after all. And so, I sang during the day and threw great stones into the lake. And by night, between naps, I sang old pirating songs most lustfully, booming my voice into the mountains and slammed rocks against one another in accompaniment. I missed sorely the cups of rum to wet my whistle, but I made do with lake water. I made such a racket that I was quite sure that any living thing within earshot of my personal orchestra would have wished my demise. The thought of this made me bellow with such laughter that my sides hurt and the mountains echoed. My efforts were not for nought. One radiant night, as I sang at the top of my lungs into a phosphorescent and sparkling heavens, I heard a yowling roar roll through the mountains. My game of psychological warfare was working. But to my quick dismay, I then heard another voice in the dark, from another mountainside, roar in response. It seemed that I had thoroughly irritated not one, but two of the Yeti. Now that could prove to be problematic. I faltered for a moment, perhaps my plan was working too well. How many of the Yeti might I attract with my efforts? I paused, thinking things through. Then proceeded again with a renewed gusto. Come one, come all. A most grand battle it would be. I laughed uproariously at the thought of doing battle with many of the Yeti; my laughter was immediately met with such a cacophony of enraged vocalizations thundering through the mountains that my very bowels vibrated. This would be fun. I laughed again, only louder. I soon grew bored of my tiny island as I waited for my transformation. I had by this time consumed every mussel that I could find, had scraped off all of the algae and gulped it down, and had drunk enough lake water for a lifetime. I could hardly wait for battle. I walked obsessively in circles around the island and shouted pirate profanities into the mountainsides. I thirsted for blood. I desired the sound of crunching bones beneath my fearsome teeth. I longed for the swift death of my enemies. At times, I questioned whether the Yeti would not swim across to kill me before my transformation had begun. But they seemed to be most averse to the water. A good thing, that. At long last, the full moon presented herself. That silver-white goddess of my accursed existence. Yet I welcome her. Always welcome her. An excited joy rises tickling in my heart at the sight of her. I had long adored her, then long despised her. Either way,

I have always welcomed her. I could not but do otherwise. The Moon Goddess had presided over my transformation on that fateful night on the Sicilian seashore. She is woven into my being, my soul, just as the saltwater. I am of her very essence, and she of mine. The elders luminesce because of her, they generate moonlight in their veins and it illuminates their skin. I have begun to notice her light glowing from within me as well. I had once thought that perhaps bioluminescent algae were responsible for this, they are not, it is her power transmitted to us during inception and through us in mature transformation that makes this possible. Yet she is a cold god. A god of cold light. And we are cold too. She reflects a cold light and we produce a cold light. How strange that is. An illusion almost. Yet we are real. She is real. The light is real. We are both the mirror and the reflection, but we are not that which is reflected. We are something else. Neither fully of this world, nor fully removed from it. We live in the space between worlds. Though our actions are of this one. My pained reverie was interrupted by the shriek of a Yeti and I snapped back into the present. Aye, time for battle. I felt the transformation begin. I stripped and jumped into the lake, soon fully transformed, I felt the hysterical joy of possessing such an extreme of power that danger was welcomed and fearsome creatures sought after. I broke the surface and swam towards the shore, my dorsal fin quivering with anticipation. It was time to have some fun. I swam to the shore and crawled up just enough to ensure that I could be seen. I then thrashed my tale and bellowed with the odd hiss that came with my voice as a wereshark. Waited. Did the same again. And slid back into the water and away from the shore. It took only a few more moments and I saw the Yeti and then another and another, until I counted five of them scouting in a frenzy about the shoreline where I had just been. I had not expected this. More than one, yes, but not five. No matter, I was in my element and could stay there for days snacking on mountain trout. I slapped my tale and submerged then surfaced nearby and did the same again, this time moving in close to the shore. The first Yeti that I dragged beneath the water had begun to wade in a little, up to its knees, looking for whatever had made the sounds in the lake. They seemed to have deduced that it was me but had no inkling that I had set a trap for them nor for what lay in store for them. I liked to think that this one was my previous aggressor. I sprang out of the water and caught the Yeti by the neck between my great jaws. Its power was immense and only the element of surprise and my wicked teeth sunk deep and full into its neck had allowed me to pull it headlong into the water using my very substantial bodyweight and the great power of my tale anchored between the rocks at the lake bottom. It thrashed at me as I pulled it forward and the pain that I felt surprised me a little, it then tried to bear hug me hoping to break my spine, but my dorsal fin blocked its attempt and anyway it was too late, I had it beneath the surface now and it stood no more chance against me than a fly in an archerfish's mouth. I ripped its neck from between its head and shoulders, spitting its larynx towards the shore where it splatted against a rock with great force and a moment later slid into the water, floating like a gruesome water lily in the shallows. The other Yetis had swarmed the spot of the attack and shrieking like enraged apes, emitted great hoots of rage, beat their chests and hopped madly about. They desired bloody vengeance. I grinned a toothy grin wide. I violently churned my tail in the water and bellowed a hissing profanity, this captured their attention. Within moments they were hurling small boulders in my direction. Their strength and speed were astounding and the volume of very large stones raining down upon me required swift maneuvering to avoid, though one did glance my dorsal fin. I went deep and swam away from the shoreline, resurfacing a safe distance away. This would be interesting. I snapped up a trout and enjoyed my snack while attempting to divine a course of action. It seemed that I might be well and truly stuck . . . in a lake . . . in the Himalayas of all places. Centuries sailing the Seven Seas, the pirate scourge of all who dared set ship to saltwater, the Red Captain himself, trapped here, in what was little more than a seasonal frog pond on the side of a mountain. I laughed uproariously at the cruel humor of it. It was no less than what I deserved. Such an undignified end this would be for the great and feared Devil of the Sea. My laughter incited the still vocally indignant Yetis to attain such a roaring and sustained crescendo of rage that I could see the sound waves rippling through the water around me. I could feel their acoustic expression vibrating my dorsal fin as though it were a harp string. Moments later, a most unexpected solution to my dilemma presented itself, as first came a crack of thunder, or so it seemed, followed quickly by the unmistakable rumbling of an avalanche rushing down the mountainside. The Yetis fled for their hairy lives in a pandemonium of shrieks and great, bounding strides while I dove deep, swimming away along the bottom of the lake. I spent the next couple of days in transformation still, eating copious quantities of trout and splicing their skins together with their bones in many criss-crossed layers. With the full moon waning and my transformation having come to its conclusion, I ventured out of the water, covering my head and body in my new fish skin cloak and having also tied layers of their skins around my feet, set off down the mountain for the nearest village. I saw neither hide nor hair of the Yetis and was right glad of that. They are a most fearsome and cunning creature and not one that I will choose to pursue again as I am at a most profound disadvantage in their habitat. I was fortunate to have escaped from their clutches. But I had wanted most desperately to see the Yeti—the Abominable Snowman, and it is that to be certain—and now I have. As I mentioned earlier, I have also done battle with the Sasquatch. In truth, it would tell much similar to this experience—they being of the same family of creature—and I was saved once again by my most fortunate proximity to water. It was then that I made the wise decision to stop seeking battle with creatures in their own habitat. It was foolhardy to take such risks for no other reason than my own entertainment. I would continue to expedition deep into remote lands on my various adventures but being sure to stay near bodies of water when at all possible and to refrain from seeking out encounters with dangerous creatures most vile. I would then, behave as though I were a risk-averse mortal. This was a blow to my inflated sense of self, but it was shrewd policy for longevity as I had finally come to understand that on land I was quite literally a fish out of water and should therefore take the precautions of one. You must understand, I am fearless when doing battle with an opponent who is physical in nature, flesh and blood and bone are my great delight. But I am as much a clucking chicken as any mortal when it comes to the supernatural, the paranormal. Yes, I am a werecreature, but I am no ghost, no angry spirit, and though I refer to myself as being a pale demon of the depths and of the deep, I use such descriptions figuratively, for I am far from being a demon. I have encountered such, and I am not that. I enjoyed being called the Devil of the Sea, it was a fair and accurate description of my nefarious exploits upon the high seas. I was a pirate after all, and more wicked than any before or since, but I am no devil of the spirit realm, nor of the spiritual one, only of the physical. I am of this world as we know it to be, and though I am very different from you, the laws of nature still ultimately apply to me.

And so, I make no bones about my fear of the supernatural. And though I may be considered a supernatural being myself, which would be true in a sense, I am not that sort of supernatural entity. I am sure that you understand my meaning. It is okay that you might think less of me for my cowardice in this matter. I have nothing to prove and no reputation to uphold. At least no longer, though I once did. And I would add—it is not my intention to disquiet you—that if you were to have been of the mind to insinuate that such be the case in my earlier years, I would have run you through with my cutlass before the words that I saw forming in your eyes made it to your lips. For the perception of my bravery had to be absolute and beyond reproach, with my crew foremost and with all others too. It is good then that we are here now and better yet even that we be on our respective sides of this page . . . mayhap I have written myself into a mood most morose.

Forgive me, dear reader, old honor dies hard. It is like a hot acid that I feel in my veins at such moments. Let me make amends with you by telling another tale, no, let me tell you two tales more. And since we are on the subject, let it be about ghosts then.

~ VI ~

THE WONDERWORKER

This first tale involves a woman who was a famed practitioner of the séance. Her name was known throughout Europe and even in the colonies of the New World. She held high society by the very gasp in its lungs, and when she saw fit to relinquish her grasp, they would only then exhale and breathe once more. She reaped great wealth through her enterprise of mediumship. A pirate of the levitating table and a scurvy scallywag if ever there was one. As fortune would have it, she was the passenger of a great ship upon which we had taken boarding action to secure. With hooks and grapnels we boarded and fought melee combat till we took the ship and all its rich booty. Young Teach was by my side, lifetimes before he would become known as Blackbeard—Scourge of the Seven Seas and the captain of my own true ship given, the *Ximena Feroz*. We found the spiritualist hiding in a place most apropos: under a table and its draping cloth in the ship's ballroom. We politely attempted to help her from her hiding place, but upon glimpsing our bloodied, sooty and sunburnt faces, she shrieked in such a profound cataclysm of terror that poor young Teach tripped backwards in surprise and landing on some large, plush piece of furniture, demolished it with such a swift efficiency and in such an explosion of flying sticks and wooden pegs that I ignited with roaring laughter, spraying the still flowing battle-blood from my mouth across the bottom of the now utterly hysterical psychic's dress and across the tops of her fine boots. This did little to soothe her fragile emotional state and her shrieking instantly intensified to such an alarming pitch that I became concerned as to her odds of surviving herself. A moment later she fainted and more's the better that was, thank Neptune. Upon her revival, we stayed in the ballroom and I had young Teach fetch a bottle of rum and two cups, three lit candles, my smoking pipe with a pouch of Virginia tobacco and a new journal, quill pen and inkwell. I had two of my men posted just outside the door and young Teach seated nearby as a witness to the event and as a spy for any tricks that might be tried should they escape my notice. I intended to leisurely and dutifully record this wily woman's spiritualist performance for my future study in such arcane matters. I made no pretense of my skepticism and bid her begin her show when she felt sufficiently inspired to do so. A third cup of rum seemed to carry with it the necessary and sufficient inspiration. She began. And I had seen it all before. Dim candlelight, strange vocalizations and cheap parlor tricks and theatrics. See the table rise? Foot beneath the leg. Yawn. I was growing bored.

Young Teach was growing drowsy. The bottle of rum was empty. My tobacco almost gone. I had not even put quill to ink or opened my journal. I gruffly thanked the spiritualist—who glared at me contemptuously—and commanded young Teach to bring her to her quarters. An odious trickster that woman. I would think on it no more. I gathered my items and walked slowly back to what had been the captain's quarters. It had been a long day. We plundered and sold the ship, ransomed the prisoners and set sail for the Galápagos Islands. It was my intention that we should enjoy a well-earned rest and further bolster our stores of freshwater and provision some turtle meat. We stayed a glorious fortnight and set sail back into the open ocean. One night, after having completed the day's entry in my captain's log—yes, even a pirate captain keeps a log, I am not entirely a wild man of the sea—I decided that I should like to write some maritime poetry. I poured a cup of rum and opened my journal. The very same I'd had with me during the clairvoyant's performance and as you may recall, it being new and unused. But when I opened it, there I saw writing, and as I leafed through it I saw that not a page remained blank, all having been written upon. I began reading from the start and such a tale was told that it shivered my very being. Here was the tale of a woman born thousands of years ago in Mesopotamia, who was to become a high priestess, her powers most remarkable and such that she subdued the priests arrayed against her in a struggle for control of their already ancient religion, and its holy places and centers of power. Their god, a true fire god, predating and at least as powerful as Ahura Mazda of Zorastrianism for whom fire was more a symbol than a god essence—and far more so than Svarozhits the Slavic fire god, who though important was but a local deity and not the ruler of a cosmic domain. And unlike the Zoroastrians, fire itself was indeed that which the adherents of her religion worshipped. Fire the razer. An all-powerful and all-consuming natural force that both killed and gave renewed life, that cleansed, that destroyed; that swept bare all through which it blazed, leaving a profusion of new life after it. She was a thaumaturge, a wonderworker of the highest possible order. Some might call her a sorceress, but that would not provide any real measure or comprehension of the powers that she possessed. She wielded magic as none had before and that none have since. She was nearly immortal and eventually would have become fully so. Nearly a demigod. She directed the rise and fall of empires, routed great armies, fought back invading demonic forces arriving in this dimension and the ancient evils that would bring with them death and famine and pestilence. She was loved and she was feared. But there came a time when she no longer wished to exist in this realm. She sought her cosmic ascendancy elsewhere. She was evolving beyond this world. And so she chose to sacrifice herself to the fire god. To become one with the source of her grand powers. She made her way to Pompeii, surrounded by thousands upon many thousands of her acolytes who threw rose petals before her, such that she took nary a step that was not so cushioned. She had climbed Mount Vesuvius, had spoken a prayer of lightning in the voice of thunder, and had serenely committed herself to the lava lake. Soon after, a great sphere of fire was said to have risen from the caldera, growing into a flowering tree of fire that later swirled into itself to become an amorphous cloud of fire, finally blossoming as a fire lotus that vanished slowly into the uppermost reaches of the sky. The world trembled when she left it. And the gods shed their tears upon the lands. She was never to return. I finished reading and put the journal down. I could feel my brain pulsing electric with amazement. If this tale were true, then it would rewrite the very history of religion. How did it come to be in my journal? It was bewildering. Could the charlatan spiritualist have managed to pull off such an audacious trick as that, right before my eyes and those of young Teach as well? And if so, how did she come by this tale? Had she become the channel for it? I sat in a state of dazed and transfixed reverie, pondering this strange and most unexpected glimpse into the unknown. A great mystery. It confounds me still. And I'll not find the answers I seek. This upsets me. Mysteries fascinate and frustrate me in equal parts. Ah, but forgive me, I no longer feel like telling the second tale. Maybe later. I hope this one will suffice for the time being, though not a ghost story at all, really. Anyway, I wish to speak of other things now. You will permit me this latitude, will you not? Does this make me an unreliable narrator? I think not, for my tales are as true in their reckoning as nautical twilight. I am though, most mercurial and of an incandescent inspiration. This next reminiscence should be of interest. Though it may pertain to the earthly, it holds some weight of the celestial. While traveling through my beloved Italy, I had found the famed *lapis solaris,* the extraordinary stone that emits light, in an ancient Benedictine monastery in the foothills of the Apennines. Guarded by this ferocious yet scholarly order of monks who would die every man jack in the cause of its protection, I managed to convince them that I would be a righteous custodian of the stone; a persuasion facilitated in no little measure by my transference of an absolutely staggering sum to the cash-strapped holy order. I hold it to this very day and it is one of my most prized possessions. It has brought me joy and comfort these many years long, like bottles of rum and of red wine. It is a most remarkable stone that emits light seemingly of its own accord. I have read by it when no candles were available to me. Its light produces a field of immensely harmonious tranquility that I enjoy immeasurably. It is light of a magical quality and though science sought to explain the mechanism of this emission of light from a stone—what a strange thing—and eventually succeeded in doing so, it was not nor will it ever be able to explain its essence. Science falls short of measuring the whole in all of that which it seeks to describe, as it captures only some aspect of a thing, while missing the others. Nonetheless, science is an invaluable tool and is the reason we no longer burn women at the stake as witches and exhaust ourselves—even paralyze ourselves—with a heavy catalog of superstitions carried like a spiteful monkey on our back. Though it is a tool with certain limitations, it is far superior to the tyranny of superstition. Still, I chuckle when I think of some of these. Like the men somewhere in Asia—could it have been Indonesia? I do not recall—who tie a heavy object to their physical qualification during some particular time of the year, believing that the season of demons is upon them once more, during which said qualification is made to disappear bit by terrible bit. Oh, the horror. But back to the story at hand. On many occasions, I have come to as though at the snap of a hypnotist's fingers and found that I have been staring at the stone, so utterly absorbed by its properties of luminescence that I have lost all track of time and all awareness of my surroundings. A potentially fatal lapse in my vaunted defense. Albeit this only happens in my stronghold as that is the only place in which I will allow myself the luxury of relaxation, more a self-indulgence, really, of which the stone is one element of my regimen. It is almost like a television for me and I am drawn to it like a moth to a flame as I drink deep into my cups. I have noticed that upon waking—I will call it that—from these mesmerized states, I have recall of things that I am not at all sure that I have in fact seen. Though it is easy enough to convince myself that I must have. Why not? After all, I have seen a great many things. A product of age is a blurring together of one's memories. While some stay fresh and vivid, others fade into the spectral, images become echoes, a strangeness indeed. I am many hundreds of years old now. And though immortal, I am not entirely immune to the ravages of time. I awoke from one these of stone-induced trances with my mind awash in images of sharks swimming in a red glow about underwater magma vents. These volcano sharks are very much a real phenomenon, but when did I see them exactly? I am not sure. At other times, the images from the stone awaken me in a fright, lurching for my cutlass and pistols, my eyes come into focus and I begin to surface in my wakefulness, but a great sense of unease and unsettled anxiety pervades my being. It is at these times that I wonder if the stone is not some sort of conduit for strange energies, a portal to other realms and other possibilities. I love that stone but have at times considered returning it to those formidable monks in the Apennines. I hope that they have not become hedonistic and possibly even debauched with their extensive wealth, instead using it to sharpen the blade of their spiritual steel. It will be one or the other. I am curious which it is but will not visit them to find out. I am afraid as to what I might find. Now, as has always been, we need righteous warriors to do battle with the many creeping evils that crawl across our lands and beset us from all sides. I say us, but really I mean you, the good of heart. I am too far wicked now to ever again include myself in the tally of the just. The Devil will come if you but call his name. I have done so on more occasions than I care to remember. It was an integral facet of my strategy of terror upon the high seas. Ah, well, a fool was I. Am I. Will I ever be. And a wicked one. Albeit with a strict code of pirate honor broken only during my bouts of near-raving madness upon the waves of the open ocean. I don't call it lunacy, as I am of the moon and lunacy goes but a little way in describing my condition during those storms of severe mood. But wicked, nonetheless. And I would prefer to assign that fault to being a wereshark. It's easier that way, isn't it? Easier than taking any personal responsibility for being a wicked creature. Oh? Do I sound a bit like everyone else? Of course I do. We clamber to blame our failings on anything but ourselves don't we? Go ahead, look in the mirror. There you go. Be truthful with yourself. You have found your answer. Have you not? Just as I have, but with longer, so much longer to reflect upon my own reflection. Now what will you do with this knowledge? Be honest. The stone has shown me more visions than I could possibly find the inclination to retell. It has shown me the very history of Western civilization—and beyond. The triumphs and the sheer greatness and the madness and the beauty and the carnage and abject ruin of it all too. It has shown me the Great Library of Alexandria burning, a tragedy that made my very guts writhe. It has shown me the many battles of the Greco-Persian Wars between the Achaemenid Empire and the Greek city-states. It has shown me Hannibal on his great elephant drive, marching to lay siege to Rome. It has shown me heroic naval battles upon the Mediterranean Sea between the Phoenicians and the Greeks that

raged my blood and made me roar with that most exquisite of sensations, the battle lust that burns at the top of
one's head and unifies the entirety of one's being into
a singular and defined purpose. It was during these visions of the stone, that I would destroy entire swaths of
my great study believing myself to be in battle upon the
sea and would send the terrified servants scurrying for
safety just as quickly as they'd arrived I'm told. I have driven my cutlass through many a leather recliner, no, not
many a servant, is that what you were thinking I would
write? And I have laughed in disbelief at the mayhem I
have inflicted on my own library and my most treasured
collections of antiquities in these fits of the stone. Such
strange effects. I have in fact wondered if it might be the
Stone of Knowledge, providing that substance called the
philosopher's stone long sought after by the ancient al-
chemists. Transmutation and transformation being as es-
sential to their enterprise as my own. Maybe it was fated
that this odd stone should come into my possession. After all, I am a living alchemy of the night sea and of the
full moon and of dark, unknown magics. I am as much a
mystery as any of the mysteries with which I obsess myself. And maybe that is the answer in and of itself. That I
seek myself in the pursuit of the other. Looking outside of
myself when I should only be looking inwardly. In these
moments of introspection, I reach for the rum. Self-real-
ization can be much overrated I have found. In truth, so
too the soothing mitigation of the rum. It falls far short.
When the wound engulfs the bandage whole, there is lit-

tle to be done I'm afraid. It was in these very moods that I would leave my quarters and terrorize my crew upon the high seas. I had many games to play. Sometimes I would call to have a rope tied round a lad's ankles and winched up to the crosstrees of the topmast, whereupon another lad took hold of a second rope tied round the wrists of the one aloft and would proceed to propel the rope in a robust, corkscrewing motion. My entertainment was attempting to shoot the first rope. Which I often enough did. Young Teach always protested such cruelties, much to his good testament. I once pushed him partially over the gunwale and held him there, hand around throat, having tired of his pestering voice of conscience. Yet, and this was what made me most morose, I knew him to be right in these matters. And it made me feel all the more vile and at odds with myself and with what I hoped my true self to be. I will always appreciate his forgiveness of my many evils. Of my evil. And the forgiveness of my right fearsome crew. I always made it up to them tenfold in the end, nay a hundredfold. And saved so very many more of their lives in battle than I ever took in my madnesses. Aye. This they would not have argued. And though their captain now be otherworldly, they are still my dread crew and will be forevermore. Nothing can change that, not even death itself. Though it may try. And one lovely day, when at long last we are reunited—for that day will come, I am sure of it—there will be a new dread lord of the dark and otherworldly high seas and it will be once more as it once was. And as though it always were. This I know. Bless you mates, we'll meet again. I grow weary of my loneliness. No man is an island though I long fancied myself to be one. I was wrong. I have come to understand that none of this really means anything without one's fellows.

But what of the afterlife? Will there be one for me? Though there be some shadow of a doubt in my mind, I think that there will be. For I am quite sure that I will not in actuality live forever. Yes, I am immortal, but am I truly? Does that make sense? Will I indeed live indefinitely? I do not think so. Will I live until the sun burns itself to a red giant billions of years from now? Very likely engulfing the earth, or at the very least boiling its seas away. Would I be able to survive that? I hardly think so. If humans had long since vanished from this world, imagine my lonely solitude. Or if they had become a space-faring race, star travelers, would I have gone with them as the sun began its growing pains? Imagine a wereshark on a starship. That would prove to be most problematic. And billions of years later, when the sun becomes a white dwarf, would I return to earth to see what might be left of it? Would I become a starship captain eternally sailing the celestial seas? Would I chart new passages forevermore and alone, through the most distant reaches of the cosmic ocean vast? I know not. But imagine the things that I would see. Such spectacles of the physical universe to behold. Would I eventually come to a place of nothingness? A place where the universe has not yet expanded into? What then? And would that even be possible? What do we really know? To entertain such notions is to wander within a great and bewildering phosphorescence of the mind—an afterglow of thought that illuminates the short path to madness.

Ah, but I have drunk too much as I write this. We will continue refreshed another time then. I wish you a restful sleep and bid you a good night.

~ VII ~

DREAD LORD OF
OTHERWORLDLY SEAS

And so. I have seen much that I will tell you, but few things can match fully the emerald-green dragon of the Caspian Sea. I first saw this grand sight on an expedition to the great inland sea, surrounded by countries of such ancient history that the air felt heavy with it. I cannot describe it otherwise. History has a physical weight, which pervades the atmosphere as though written upon the air in such environs. We often think of dragons as land-dwelling creatures, who are especially particular to mountainous regions. But this dragon was born of the sea. A sea dragon as it were. It lives deep beneath the depths of the Caspian, in an ancient and long-submerged megalithic structure of such immense and expansive architecture that it makes me quite certain that giants once inhabited this world, as has been attested to by many sources, with their handiwork being the ultimate advertisement of their existence. How such came to rest beneath these waters is not known to me, but perhaps to the dragon that resides there still, though I have yet to ask it of this. I was able to befriend the dragon and I pay it a visit from century to century in transformation. It views me to be a most unusual lifeform, a strange specimen any werecreature is and perhaps more so a wereshark. It enjoys my companionship, brief and seldom as it may be. Its proper name is Veles, so named the dragon has told me, after a Slavic chthonian deity and psychopomp, ruler of the underworld, who is represented as a zmey or Slavic dragon, which Veles is some form of and strangely enough, we became friends almost immediately upon encountering one another deep in the Caspian. The dragon had been swimming slowly, shimmering in an emerald-green glory in the dimly lit depths and when it saw me—attempting to leave quickly and unseen—it roared a great bubbling sound—thankfully, a greeting as it turned out—in an ancient tongue I had never heard before. I had stopped, caught like a child with his hand in the cookie jar, not knowing at all what to do. This seemed to amuse the great beast and it roared more bubbles, but in these sounds I could detect humor and knew them to be laughter. I turned and grinned a toothy grin, whereupon the dragon laughed its bubbles even more uproariously and in turn, I too began to laugh, nervously at first. And so it was. We were friends. Such tales this ancient being has told me. Of strange races of men that no longer walk this earth and who possessed powers and technologies that we would still call magic in this day and age. And visitations to this world by those from other worlds. Who came to be represented as sky gods and saintly entities, their helmets as halos, their weapons as bolts of lightning, their spacecraft as stars, their technology as miracles. And of forces both of good and of evil, in a perpetual war, that have laid waste the human populations and the flora and fauna of entire continents during their battles that manifested in this dimension. Some of these devastations might seem to be attested to by the great swaths of radioactive dead zones deep in the geological record that have supposedly been found by some and interpreted as such by those same. Veles confirmed that all that which we call myths, are largely truth but for a little extra polish on them from the many retellings. It was during one of these conversations that I learned the answer to my curiosity of how the dragon's palace of stone came to be under the sea. It had been atop a high hill, but a great flood had swept across the earth, wiping from its face the megalithic cultures that had built such things. This had once been a great valley, which then became a great, inland sea. Veles had for millennia untold lived beneath the waters of the Black Sea, but upon one of its frequent expeditions in search of treasure on land and in sea, had found this aquatic estate much to its liking and has now been its inhabitant for many millennia. The dragon still visits its great treasure trove beneath the Black Sea from time to time but has no interest in moving those riches from one sea to the next. It has stated that it took quite long enough to get all of it there in the first place and that anyway, its new nest has grown to be quite significant. It seems to view its Black

Sea abode as something of a pied-à-terre for its various excursions throughout its old haunts and the Mediterranean. Veles is attended to by a legion of Nereids and a species of elf that lives in the sea. I had known little about these elves prior, they seem to be a good enough lot. The sea nymphs are most glorious to behold and can be very kind, but Neptune save your hide should ye be fool enough to cross one. They are not to be trifled with. I once saw them take down a sea troll in the shallows of the Baltic Sea just off the coast of Latvia long ago. They used his war hammer as a lever to unhinge his jaw atop his neck in much the same fashion that one uses a bottle opener. I would say now that his head swung back like the top of a Pez dispenser. And jamming their Triton's trumpet down his throat, they jumped in such a wrathful frenzy upon the poor chap's great barrel of a chest that there sounded a long series of conch blasts, concluding with one last hissing honk like that of a goose. I chuckled at the musical mayhem, making a mental note of Nereid ferocity and of the importance of courtesy when addressing them and of the quick fatality of drawing too near them when not invited to do so.

One other fiendish torture that I will mention purely for the historical record as this is my memoir after all and so I do not feel that I should knowingly withhold from you, my dear reader, memories that might flash across my mind like silver fish in moonlit pools. I had a very large magnifying glass—fit for any giant—made to order in Belgium. Initially, I had intended to use it to study jars of sea water, to see what I might see. But soon enough, I had devised other uses for it, which, in truth, had been long in the pondering before its crafting, but I had very much enjoyed the fiction of stating that it would be used for scientific purposes. A captain of science, I. Aye. Like Darwin himself. But it was only a vulgar fiction. My dread bones had been wrought for other purposes. Dark deeds done with the cutting edge of my cutlass should qualify as a form of scientific discipline for their quick precision in dispatching the subjective falsities of the human mind and arriving at the objective truth of one's own mortality. But alas they do not. Perhaps in the midst of some inner doldrums with no ships to plunder, no pirating prize to capture, I would be able to strike an inquisitive spark in the melancholy of a mood and following that light, use the magnifying glass for scientific observations. But on no occasion did that happen. Rather, I had a very large and heavy table made with the middle portion cut away and reinforced about its lengths. Onto this structure the magnifying glass with its quite substantial weight was placed. A canvas tied round it so that it would not burn a hole through the ship's hull on a bright and sunny day. But burning a hole through another ship's hull was another matter indeed. And this I tried on occasion with the glass contained in another contraption, a vertical mechanism on wooden wheels, but the constant movement of the sea, fluctuating distances and duration required were such that it simply did not work, even on the sunniest of days. However, utilizing the table I found another use for the great glass, a most satisfying one, during one of my madnesses. In this application the magnifying glass proved most efficient. Exceptionally so, in fact. I would have prisoners roped by the wrists and ankles and dragged beneath the great glass, my crew holding fast the four ends. The canvas was removed and my entertainment began. Scorching a man's innards with such a device takes not very much longer than frying a fish in a galley pan as it turns out. The trick was not to burn clean through in a sustained manner lest the planks beneath were to suffer much the same fate. Though I tried, it however did not work for shrinking a human head into a tsantsa as the Shuar tribe of the Ecuadorian Amazon were once most fond of doing, as the requirements of that particular undertaking did not allow for deviation from its precise and long-established processes. My clever instrument entertained me during the course of several madnesses before being washed overboard one foul night during a violent storm with a gale wind, much to my annoyance. I did not have another one made as it would have been a great inconvenience to do so and as it did require a full-bright sun to work as I meant it to, which proved to be a great source of frustration for me on more than one occasion.

I have seen the kaleidoscope of beauty that is the expression of the light of the sun and of the moon upon the sea. I have seen light pillars that shone with the radiance of a cosmic sun as though from between the great branches of Yggdrasil itself. And sun dogs that bedeviled my very senses. Alpenglow though a phenomenon of the high mountains is the same that I have seen upon the great clouds that appear as mountain ranges at sea. So, too, Brocken spectres when the sun would pierce the clouds and the shadow of the lookout aloft in the mainmast loomed giant in its projection upon the sea mist. A shadow giant. I have seen Ulloa's halo—the white rainbow or fog bow—and I have seen great arches of white light reflecting the moonlight. The sea is a mystical place and as beautiful as it is deadly.

I have enjoyed the city of Venice more than any city on the face of the earth. That grand city of the lagoon. A city upon the water. Within the water. Beneath the water. Surrounded by water. Slowly sinking and crumbling into the water. Such history it holds. Such ghosts rising evaporative from the lagoon through the floors above to haunt the palazzos. I have enjoyed swimming its canals and exploring the twilight waters beneath its structures in long meditations of study. Ancient foundations long submerged. Such a marvel this city. Such a feat of determination. It is fascinating to see the evolution of the architectural efforts and buoyant technologies employed throughout the city's long history to keep it from sinking into the bottom of the lagoon. Its systems of pontoons do much to keep it afloat. Venice is akin to a ship in the water. So strange to swim beneath a city. To watch the fireworks from the Grand Canal during the many festivals is a pleasure, though it must be similar to having gone overboard during a battle at sea with muskets and great canons firing overhead. But nothing can compare with the entertainment of tormenting the Venetian gondoliers and their passengers. Such fun bumping the bottoms of the gondolas, just enough to gain the attention of its passengers. Just enough to concern them. I usually refrain from tipping the whole lot into the water. But biting a forcola in half and watching its poor gondolier fall flailing into a canal has amused me greatly on more occasions than I can recall. The look on their faces when they see me in the cloudy water, lurking just beneath the surface, has provided me with more laughter even than the surfers that I terrorize off the coasts of every continent.

I remember this story only because of the song a fisherman sang as I slowly approached his little craft, stopping a short distance from it. I had heard his song from beneath the waves and had surfaced to see who it belonged to. The song was an odd one, mayhap the invention of the man himself. I listened intently from among the waves and upon its conclusion, chose to spare him and find my supper elsewhere. It seems more the song of a woodsman than a fisherman. Maybe that is why he sang it. I have written the words of his song for you here.

Sweet shadow jamboree
Cold wind blowing through the leaves
Moonlight shining from just above the trees
So good to feel free
So good just to be
Down through the hollow I do see
You riding that pale shadow horse up for me

So good to feel free
So good just to be
You'll be here soon
Pale shadow woman in the light of the moon
You are not what I thought you to be
Long ago
So long ago
So good to feel free
So good just to be
Pale shadow woman on a pale shadow horse
Pale shadow woman
Just a moment longer
To finish this bottle
Of mountainberry wine
To finish this bottle
Though I know, I know it now
Been coming for a long, long time
Sweet shadow jamboree
Up through the hollow
Pale shadow woman
Riding up for me
Fast as the cold wind, riding up for me
Cold wind blowing through the leaves
Moonlight shining from just above the trees
From just above the trees
That pale shadow woman
Is coming for me
Coming for me

As I swam away, the fisherman in the boat caught sight of my dorsal fin and fired a shot with his rifle, which struck its target—much to my irritation. Understand that it takes far more than that if one hopes to inflict even the mildest of injuries upon me. He was a good and quick shot, I'll give him that. My temper rose not because of the bullet, but because unbeknownst to the fisherman, I had spared his life. I had chosen not to kill him for my supper. It would have taken but an instant. How fortunate he would have considered himself if he had only known. But he did not. Such dumb impudence is a thankless impudence, nonetheless. I would not spare the insufferable bastard twice. The old adage that no good deed goes unpunished is apropos here I think. I had cleaved his boat in two halves before he could blink. They sank on either side of him as he floundered in shocked disbelief. Horror came but a moment later. Oh, how quickly the tables had turned he may have thought if he'd only had the time. Though in truth his death had become an inevitability when first I heard his song. But neither of us yet knew it to be so. The Fates wrote it in steaming ink as he sang and Death took cold notice. I had simply granted him a momentary reprieve. I cleaved him in half as well. Snapping into him as a bear trap would. His intestines popped as a symphony of overripe tomatoes and as I swam away, they unraveled as a ball of yarn does, a bloody mass of it, some end or other stuck between my teeth. I would find my supper elsewhere when my mood had improved. I sang his song as I swam and committed it to memory. An odd song.

I am sure that you are well acquainted with the legend of the ghost ship called the *Flying Dutchman*. I can tell you that it is not a legend, though it has indeed become legendary. My own ship's encounter with this spectacle of the supernatural is one that bewilders me to this day. My crew and I, as was true of most seafarers of our day, were well aware of the strange tale of the *Flying Dutchman* and of its many purported sightings. The day of our encounter had begun like any other. It had stopped raining and the clouds settled atop the sea as a thick and rolling fog. I had retired to my cabin for a hot toddy and some reading. No sooner had I removed the book from its shelf than I'd heard the warning cry of the lookout. Upon taking the deck, I saw a great and glowing ship emerging through the fog, bearing down full upon the *Ximena Feroz* intent on ramming her amidships. As I gave the order to come about, our spectral foe gained such a burst of speed as to blur its lines. We had barely just begun to maneuver when it rammed us. Or should have. And the *Ximena Feroz* and all aboard would have been sent down to Davy Jones' Locker. But nothing happened. Neither to my ship nor to my crew. My memory is vivid in this matter. I had watched in frozen horror as the ship passed through my own, like any ship would cut through a fog at sea. And then it was gone. I saw no captain and no sailors aboard the vessel and heard no sound. It vanished into the fog itself just as a fog vanishes into the air itself. A moment later, the realization of what we had just seen dawned upon us each and every one and we stood long in a ponderous silence, battling our superstitions and grappling heavily with the chilling experience. I never saw the *Flying Dutchman* again and more's the better. But for a long while after, I very much expected to see it again, devoid of any living soul aboard, bearing down upon us at a preternatural speed through a fog—and just as silent as any—or in the still of night when the many realms of haunted possibilities manifest themselves most energetically.

Ah, this little tale comes to me now. I will apologize in advance. In the long hours of my madnesses at sea, I have had the skins of men flown as windsocks from the yards and masts. To see the entirety of the skin of a man's body, carefully stitched to integrity, mouth wide agape, snapping and spinning aloft in the wind is an unusual and most captivating sight. With some we took less care and so headless sailors also flew above the ship. Phantoms fluttering in the wind. The skins pale under the dark clouds but aglow like paper lanterns when the sun shone through them. I can only imagine the concern of those poor souls aboard the ships we closed fast upon. Sometimes even I had them stitched onto the sails. And once had a whole sail made from the skins of my enemies, those of a particularly formidable captain and his crew. It honored their ferocity and celebrated our own. We hoisted it for the intended spectacle of fear upon our approach to a merchant ship, but it was soon in tatters.

We later threw it overboard and watched it sink ghostly beneath the waves. None of the skins lasted long in the ever-lashing elements of the sea and I soon found new entertainments. Those of my crew more sensitive to such inhumanities may have reassured themselves with the old adage that the devil you know is better than the devil you don't.

I will stop here for the time being, dear reader. I have much to attend to and especially as it pertains to an up-coming expedition and so I grow weary of telling my sto-ries. I will take this up again when feeling sufficiently inspired to do so. I have much left to tell. In truth, I have far more left to tell than has already been told. But I am sure that you have come to that realization already. I am, after all, a very old being and yet my stories—the one's I have thus far told—make only a skinny book, barely enough upon which to place your cup of Irish breakfast tea when in search of its saucer. I have alluded to a vast realm of untold stories and this I will explore with you further when the time is right. Peace be upon thee—or so those who would aspire to be a force of good in this ever-troubled world might say. Ah, such saints. Perhaps. I envy them their goodness and thank them for it and for their many and sustained kindnesses in this world we call ours. But if they be false and bereft of honor, if they be hypocrites, two-faced and foul, then I will see them in Hell when my time at long last comes and they will scrub with their bloody, shredded gums, ever drown-ing, the barnacles from beneath my true-good ship for an eternity. My many honorifics have included that of Dread Lord of the Seven Seas and Dread Lord of the High Seas. For all of this, don't you see? I am the heir apparent, my voyage has just begun. I will be anointed the Dread Lord of Otherworldly Seas. Mark my words. Let me catch them with honey on their lips and cold steel in their heart. Poison-tongued whisperers. Venomous serpents most vile. They will be made to await my arrival, knowing full well their hard penance be due, the very tax upon the luxury of their sins. Its dread collector forthcoming. My presence is no Fata Morgana of the sea. I am no apparition gliding the waves. No phantasm in the currents. I am a universal truth, come bold and vengeful for the wicked as only the very embodiment of itself can be. I am that now and forevermore. I am the self-correction. The oscillation of the pendulum. This accursed werecreature of the deep that I became on that fateful night will be reborn with a sense of divine purpose as a righteous instrument of retribution for the one, true God. As a vessel of vengeance I will live this dichotomy most joyously. A wicked one, the archnemesis of the wicked. I will be the terrible weapon forged in its own evil and wielded by its own hand. And through my wickedness I might atone in some small measure for the wicked that I have done and will continue to do. My ways will not change and my madnesses will come, my transformations will come, like the tides, washing over me. But I will now recognize my divine purpose. That is the difference. While my contempt for the human race knows no bounds, nor does my love for it. I will do what I can. That which I believe my true self to have been, some essence still, will find its redemption. My dark voyage will have its North Star as I will have my blood—in this world and the next.

Ab omni malo, líbera nos, Dómine. Amen.

From all evil, O Lord, deliver us. Amen.

Ah, but as I mentioned a bit earlier, I must conclude our story for the moment. I write this in the mountains yearning for the sea and have written more than I had intended to during this reverie and more than I really had the time for—isn't that funny?—as pressing matters demand my attention. Why do I feel compelled to tell you my story of stories? I understand it not, though it is a great joy for me, providing a sense of community, albeit indirectly, and the gift of knowledge gained through the lived experience of an elder. The ancient art of storytelling. Still, I speak of the past but must live in the now.

I bid you good day.

ABOUT THE AUTHOR

Justin T. O'Conor Sloane is an author, artist, editor, publisher and educator. He has been fascinated with science fiction & fantasy since a young lad and has been honored to publish some of the biggest names in the field. Justin's love of SFF inspired him to relaunch the classic science fiction magazines *Worlds of IF* and *Galaxy*, as well as originating various magazines, such as *The Flying Saucer Poetry Review*, the first-ever literary journal devoted exclusively to art and literature about the UFO phenomenon—his poem on this subject, "The Third Law," was a finalist for the Science Fiction & Fantasy Poetry Association's Rhysling Award. Justin won the first Macmillan Education Onestopenglish international ELT poetry contest while teaching English at the Center for Interamerican Studies in Cuenca, Ecuador. He holds an MA in educational leadership with principal certification from the University of Texas—Permian Basin and has been nominated for various teaching awards, including Humanities Texas. Justin is blessed with a wonderful and talented family and a caramel-colored dog that can sport a full mohawk from head to tail.

Thank you for purchasing this book. On the following pages a selection of some of the books and magazines published by Starship Sloane has been provided for your consideration, you can find them everywhere that great books are sold.

Visit us at starshipsloane.com and take a look around.

Safe travels, children of the stars . . .

COVER ART BY BRUCE PENNINGTON

WINTER 2023   ISSUE 2   ISSN 2770-9817

THE FLYING SAUCER POETRY REVIEW

#263
galaxy
SCIENCE FICTION
ISSN 2995-9527
Eugen Bacon
F. J. Bergmann
Eliane Boey
Ronan Cahill
A. J. Dalton
Bob Eggleton
Zdravka Evtimova
David Gerrold
Richard Grieco
Rodney Matthews
Bruce Pennington
Daniel Pomarede
Gareth L. Powell
Christopher Ruocchio
Paulo Sayeg
Robert Silverberg
Nigel Suckling
Dave Vescio

ISSN 2996-0916
WORLDS OF IF
SCIENCE FICTION
#177
Renan Bernardo
David Brin
Michael Butterworth
Tara Campbell
Kwame Cavil
A. J. Dalton
Tatiana Daubek
Bob Eggleton
Zdravka Evtimova
Richard Grieco
Akua Lezli Hope
Pedro Iniguez
Ai Jiang
Leslie Kean
Rodney Matthews
Bruce Pennington
Charles Platt
Daniel Pomarède
Paulo Sayeg
Robert Silverberg
Andrew Stewart
Nigel Suckling
Dave Vescio

praxis

David Gerrold

Foreword by John Shirley

DARK WOODS RISING

poems by
A J Dalton

HE MAY WEAR
MY SILENCE

Zdravka Evtimova

Foreword by Nigel Suckling

HAIRY HULLABALOO

poems by
RICHARD STEVENSON

illustrations by
CARLA STEIN